Captive

Companion Novel to Book 2 of The Ancestors Saga: Daughter of Ninmah

THE ANCESTORS SAGA

Exciting and compelling, *The Ancestors Saga* takes you on an epic journey 40,000 years into our own dark and forgotten past. As the world teeters on the brink of another glacial winter, homo sapiens are not the only human species to walk the Earth.

When the destiny of the entire human race hangs in the balance, the prize for survivors will be Earth itself.

The Ancestors Saga is a fantasy fiction series, a thrilling combination of history, mythology, fantasy, and adventure, retelling a lost chapter in the evolution of humankind.

ABOUT THE AUTHOR

Lori Holmes is the author of the bestselling *Ancestors Saga* and the companion series *The Raknari Trilogy*.

The idea for the Ancestors Saga first came to Lori in 2008 when her mother made a passing comment, 'what could the human race have become if only we had followed a spiritual path, rather than a technological one?' The comment set off a chain reaction. Two main characters came to life. The first was a young woman whose people had rejected technology and evolved a spiritual connection to the living world around them. The second was a man. This man was half ordinary human and half 'spiritual' human.

For a time, that was all there was, two characters sitting in a pool of light, surrounded by a mysterious darkness. This went on until one day, having a keen interest in prehistoric and ancient history, Lori was reading an article outlining evidence that our modern human ancestors interbred with the other human species we once shared our planet with. And that, as they say, is history. An ancient and icy world opened out around the two main characters, a changing world filled at once with danger and possibility, where the fate of man, in all its known and unknown forms, had yet to be decided.

Adding a dash of legend, myth, and Sumerian theories on the creation of mankind, *The Ancestors Saga* was born.

Lori's debut novel, The Forbidden, begins the epic journey into the Ancestors Saga, combining history, mystery and legend to retell a lost chapter in humanity's dark and distant past.

Lori currently lives in Shropshire, England. When not lost in the world of *The Ancestors Saga*, she enjoys spending time with her family (three children, two whippets and her husband - it's a busy house!). Lori can usually be found outdoors walking and exploring the great British countryside.

Find out more at www.loriholmesbooks.com

Also by Lori Holmes

CAPTIVE

COMPANION NOVEL TO BOOK 2 OF THE ANCESTORS SAGA: DAUGHTER OF NINMAH

LORI HOLMES

VISUAL8 PUBLISHING LTD.

CONTENTS

CHAPTER 1

FALLEN

Khalvir ran through the trees. The forest was dark, pressing in all around him as the sounds of the night roared in his ears. He was careful to keep his wits about him as he plunged through the restraining undergrowth.

This forest was not safe, filled as it was with elf mischief and magic. He could feel it, hazing across his latent inner senses, his own hated elf blood rising in answer. Khalvir quashed it viciously, before realising the sounds of his men running behind him could no longer be heard over the din of this accursed place. He had outpaced them. He gritted his teeth. It would not do to be separated. Coming to a stop beneath the overhanging branches of a thick-bodied tree, Khalvir reluctantly took a moment to steady his breath and await his fellow raiders.

He chafed at being still. It gave him too much time to reflect on the failed raid. The elf settlement had been empty, and he cursed his bad luck. His Chief would not be pleased. Each time, the Chief would send Khalvir and his men out into the forests where elves had been sighted and each time Khalvir would return empty-handed.

The Chief had made it clear that this was Khalvir's last chance and that if he failed, his displeasure would be immense. Khalvir winced beneath the spear cat skull covering his face. He had failed.

The old resentment he felt for his Chief stirred inside his chest, and he was quick to stamp on it. Khalvir struggled to understand the irrational hatred that he felt when he met those dark eyes at times. It was a feeling that had existed since their very first encounter, when he had awoken in this very forest, lost and confused, his memories stolen by the elf-witches. Khalvir blew out a breath. His Chief was hard, even brutal, but without him Khalvir would have been dead long ago. Dead at the hands of the very creatures he now sought.

True hatred blazed within his heart as he thought of the witches; murderous wood sprites that they were. He did not understand his Chief's need to possess them. Their magic was nothing but evil and trickery.

At least this raid had not been a complete waste of time. Stores of the elf-witches' food had been abandoned along with the settlement. Khalvir had ordered his men to gather as much as they could carry away, hoping such a gift would appease his Chief. The roots and fruits the elves grew in these forests were far more sustaining than anything that could be foraged out on the Plains.

Khalvir shifted uneasily beneath the tree as a prickle ran up his spine. The elves may be gone, but he couldn't rid himself of the feeling that he was being watched. It was as if their ghosts lingered, cursing him with their unseen eyes. He tightened his grip on the long curving knife in his hand. The familiar weight in his palm was reassuring. Khalvir longed for clear open spaces of the Plains where an approaching enemy could be easily detected.

At last, his men arrived. The muffled sound of footfalls and rustling leaves came first, then the puff of breath in the cool air. One by one, they emerged from the shadows and joined Khalvir under the tree. Their tense movements betrayed their own unease.

"What are we going to do, Khalvir?" Galahir's low voice sounded from beneath the great oxen skull that concealed his coarse features. Khalvir's most trusted companion's query was heavy with concern. "The Chief will not be pleased."

Khalvir sighed. "There is nothing to be done. The elves are gone. Perhaps there are no more to be found. I will be the one to inform him of the failure. No one else need share in his displeasure."

Galahir shifted as though he was about to protest, but Khalvir silenced him with a warning glance. It would be foolish to speak ill of their Chief in such company. Not all here were friends.

Khalvir glanced to where Lorhir lurked upon the edges of the group, dark and lean. That jackal would relish any opportunity to sour Khalvir's favour with their Chief. It was Lorhir's greatest ambition to see Khalvir fall from grace. Khalvir gave a soft snort. It seemed Lorhir's prayers were about to be answered.

"Rest," he told his men. "I want to be out of this forest by daybreak, and it is a long way to the borders. I dislike the feel of this place."

He was not alone in his assessment. Weary as his men were, their shadowed eyes darted beneath their varying skull masks as they sank to the ground. Khalvir was sure half of them would like to forego the respite and run until dawn, run until the trees no longer crouched over their heads, cutting off the sky, but it was unwise to deplete their energy reserves. A warrior must always have strength enough left to fight. One could never know when it might be needed.

Khalvir had just lowered himself to his haunches when it happened. A sudden snapping of wood from above shattered the silence.

Khalvir shot back to his feet, his men moving as one around him, as a high-pitched cry cut through the air.

"Nyri!"

Khalvir sucked in a breath. Two she-elves perched high in the tree above them, one dark, one silver-haired. The branch beneath the silver-haired witch had snapped, pitching her towards the ground. She clung and clawed at her companion, trying to save herself as the branch supporting her body gave way completely beneath her weight.

"No! Kyaati!" The dark-haired girl screamed in the tongue of the elves.

The heavy branch came crashing down through its brethren. Khalvir and his men scrambled back as it smashed into the earth where they had been resting. The grip of the dark-haired girl failed, and her silver-haired companion came tumbling in its wake.

Khalvir knew it was too late for her. No one could survive a fall from such a great height. The she-elf's helpless body bounced off one branch, then another. Khalvir could almost hear her bones snapping before she crumpled to the ground with a sickening thud. Her cries cut off abruptly.

For one stunned moment, no one moved. Khalvir stared at the stricken elf-witch. The quarry he had thought lost had fallen right at his feet like a gift from Ea Himself. And yet, Ea appeared to have a twisted sense of humour. He had thrown an elf to Khalvir's feet, but now the thing lay dead and broken at the base of a tree. Khalvir did not even look up to seek the other she-elf. She would be long gone, disappearing into the trees like the demon she was.

Khalvir studied the fallen creature. She had been with-child. His lips pulled back in a grimace at the double stroke of misfortune. Such a prize would have been a gift beyond his Chief's imagining. Now it was wasted to death.

Or was it? The barest of movements caught his eye, and Khalvir took a step forward. To his utter disbelief, he saw the elf-witch was still breathing. A trickle of hope cut through the gloom. If she and the infant she carried could be saved...

A cat-like snarl and a rushing of leaves was Khalvir's only warning. The dark-haired she-elf that he had all but dismissed came flying down the tree like a vengeful falcon. Her own preservation seemed to matter little to her as she threw herself recklessly to the ground to land between him and her fallen companion.

Her courage was impressive to behold. Fierce indigo eyes caught and held his. Khalvir's muscles locked down; her face stunning him into immobility. He was floating, detaching from reality. Khalvir swayed, and the elf-witch stooped to grab hold of the fallen branch. She swung it at him as he stood paralysed before her, groping for his senses as an explosion of feelings swept through him.

Or at least she tried to. The weight of the large branch proved too much for her slight body, but she fought to brandish it all the same. The aggressive action did not register. Khalvir's ears were ringing, his mind swirling. Her indigo eyes were at the centre of the maelstrom. Before he was aware of it, he stepped forward, only wanting to be nearer.

"Get away!" the elf witch hissed between her teeth.

Another step. It was as though he was being drawn by an invisible cord. Unconsciously, Khalvir lifted a hand towards her. This one was coming with them, whether she liked it or not.

"Leave her alone! Get away from us!" the elf-witch continued to screech in her peculiar tongue, but now an edge of desperation was eating away at her rage.

Khalvir's men laughed at her feeble attempts to intimidate their leader, and the harsh sound shook a sliver of reality back into Khalvir. The elf-witch bared her teeth in defiance. Khalvir took another step. Despite her bravado, she retreated.

The laughter intensified, and Khalvir felt a sudden, irrational flash of anger. This elf-witch was showing true courage. She deserved some respect. He twisted around to glare at his followers.

"Quiet!"

The laughter ebbed, and Khalvir refocused on his target. She was so close now he could almost feel her body heat against his outstretched hand. He shivered. Her glorious eyes fell on his hand and the stained knife he had all but forgotten. Khalvir watched as the strength went out of her. She knew she was defeated. Her eyes closed, releasing him from their hold.

Khalvir sucked in a breath as the spell was broken. A chill swept through him. He felt empty, humiliated, then angry as a rushing in the undergrowth reached his ears. He had been so utterly taken in that he had not realised the danger until it was too late.

A snarl ripped the air as a huge grey form burst from the trees and leapt past the girl's shoulder. The wolf stood before her, its face twisted into a grisly snarl. Khalvir cursed as another followed the first and another until fifteen forest wolves stood bristling and crouching before him and his men.

He was outnumbered and outmatched. Khalvir's mind worked furiously for a way to salvage the situation, but it was futile. Caught off guard, he was about to lose and lose badly.

Khalvir's lips pulled back from his teeth as the bitterness of defeat washed over his tongue. He knew what he must do. There was only one way to save as many of his raiding group as possible.

Without taking his eyes off the wall of teeth and fur, Khalvir gave the command that he had never before had to give.

"Run."

The answering howl split the night. His men broke and ran for their lives as the wolves charged as one. Khalvir wondered which, if any of them, would make it home.

The sour taste of defeat spread until it filled his entire mouth as the wolf pack chased down the men under his leadership.

A movement caught his eye. The witch who had defeated him had fallen to her knees. No doubt her efforts at summoning the killer beasts had drained her. Her eyes met his, somehow stealing his breath once more even amid the chaos and the screams as his men were run down and savaged. Khalvir shook his head sharply.

She had enchanted him, lured him in with her show of helplessness, and now his men were paying for his weakness with their lives. He had failed them. He had to do all he could to save them now. Khalvir tore his eyes away from the witch and fled into the trees without a backwards glance.

The dark forest blurred by as Khalvir dodged and leaped, trying to catch up to his men. He stumbled across two of them, but it was already too late. Swallowing back bile, Khalvir ran on. He had to keep moving until he was sure the wolves had given up on their pursuit. Branches whipped at him as the undergrowth sapped his strength, but still he kept going, listening for sounds of pursuit.

Then he heard it. The pounding of paws gaining fast. Khalvir increased his speed, but knew he could not outrun the beast that was closing with every stride. Unbidden, instinct took hold, and he grabbed hold of the nearest tree, scrambling up into the branches.

He wasn't fast enough.

Lupine jaws closed around his leg, ripping a cry from his throat as the wolf dragged him back down. Slammed into the earth, the sight of snapping fangs blocked out all else. Khalvir grabbed the beast about the throat, holding the teeth at bay by a hand's breadth.

His knife was tucked into his fur boot. If he tried to reach it, he was a dead man. He already was. The strength in Khalvir's arms was failing. The end was close, but he was determined to keep his eyes on the frenzied gaze of his killer until the last. He would not flinch before death with eyes closed.

And so it was that his eyes were wide open when the wolf gave a gut-wrenching howl of pain, convulsing and spattering Khalvir's face with blood before toppling to the side. Dead.

Stunned, Khalvir dropped back onto his elbows, panting with exhaustion and shock. He was alive. As a raknari warrior, he was prepared to face death whenever it came, but that did not mean he had to like it. He looked at the now lifeless wolf lying at his side and saw the spear protruding from its side in the same instant that he heard Galahir's voice calling him.

"Khalvir!"

His friend burst from the cover of the trees and ran to his side. He clamped a pale hand around Khalvir's forearm and yanked him back to his feet. Khalvir winced at his grip. Sometimes Galahir forgot he was part Thal and could crush a skull in his hands if he so chose.

"Thank you," Khalvir told him, flexing his fingers behind Galahir's back as his friend turned away to pull his spear loose from the wolf's body. The wounds the beast had dealt to his leg stung. He winced as he tested his weight upon it. It held. Just.

"I think they've stopped hunting us now," Galahir murmured.

Khalvir listened. Indeed, the forest had fallen silent around them. Too silent.

"How many lost?"

"I don't know," Galahir said. "You are the only one I have found."

Khalvir was still for a moment. The anger of his defeat burned through his chest. Beside that anger, a strange pull was growing in strength; an inexplicable compulsion to run back the way he had come.

"Khalvir," Galahir's voice shook him. "We have to get out of this forest. If any of the others survived, they will head for the borders and we can regather."

Khalvir stared into the trees. The pull was becoming a tormenting burn. Accursed indigo eyes taunted his every thought.

"Khalvir?"

Still focused on the trees, he spoke. "Go to the borders at the point where we entered. Find as many survivors as you can and then wait for me there."

"And where are you going?" Galahir eyed him warily.

"I'm going back. That elf witch and I have some unfinished business."

"Go back?" Galahir was askance. "Khalvir, they'll kill you. You cannot face them alone."

"Do as I say, Galahir." Khalvir's voice was sharp. The pull in his chest was now more than he could bear. "I will return when I have finished with her. Wait for me on the borders. Regather. Send word to the Chief of what has happened here."

"But the clan is days away!" Galahir protested.

"Send Lorhir, if he still stands."

A smile tugged at Galahir's wide lips. "You have a wicked sense of humour when you put your mind to it, Khalvir."

Khalvir grinned at him. "Go. You have charge of the men until I return."

Galahir's paled for a moment before he inclined his head and disappeared into the trees. As soon as he was gone, Khalvir let the confident smile drop from his face. He turned to the deeper forest where the indigo eyes waited, tormenting him, calling to him. Ignoring the pain in his right leg, he began to run, faster and faster as the call grew in strength. He was going to capture that witch. He was going to have his revenge for the deaths of his men. The burn in his chest blazed.

She would not even see him coming.

The sharp snapping of twigs was his only warning. Khalvir's stomach lurched as the ground gave way beneath his feet. The last thing he remembered was tumbling away into the black abyss.

Chapter 2
STRANGER

K halvir drifted, unaware of the passage of time, unable to distinguish between dreaming and awake. The light slipped in and out of the sky, unnoticed. Time was marked only by brief flashes of excruciating pain, followed by the strangest visions, when the agony chased his mind back into oblivion.

The dreams skittered. Strange half-formed pictures of a dim and forbidding forest. He heard the wind hissing through great leaves, the chatter of animals. Whispers of feeling curled through his chest like smoke in response, feelings of fear and unimaginable loss, old resentment and doubt. He shuddered away, fighting, sure the waking world of pain that waited would be preferable to these dark hauntings. He did not want to *see;* he did not want to *understand.*

Before he could escape, the musical laugh of a young girl shivered through the ghosts of his mind and the crushing sense of loss and fear lifted, banished by the brightest of lights. The trees vanished, and a pair of indigo eyes filled the entire vision.

Khalvir awoke. The dreams scattered and fled back to the deepest recesses of his mind, never to be recalled. The pain was almost enough to send him the same way. His right leg was broken and each breath he took sent jabbing pains through his chest. He wanted to give in to the darkness, to disappear again as he had so many times before, but he could not, not this time. He had to focus. His very life could depend on it. He knew instinctively what had woken him this time.

He was no longer alone.

Without opening his eyes, he breathed evenly, shallowly, so as not to aggravate whatever was broken inside. He flexed his fingers, feeling the ground beneath them. It was cold and damp and had the texture of stone.

Khalvir tensed as he detected the softest of treads. The intruder was close. He waited, still feigning unconsciousness. Whomever they were, they were hovering over him. He heard an inexplicable snort and then a soft gasp. Of disbelief? Of hope?

He was trying to decipher the meaning when he felt hands lifting the leaf leather pouch he always kept tied to his waist. Fury blazed through him at the bold intrusion. All those who knew him knew better than to touch that object. It was time to let his enemy know he was awake.

Ignoring the agony, he exploded forth, catching hold of a slender wrist and yanking it away. Quick as a cat, he threw the intruder to the rock, grabbing their throat in a choke-hold with his other hand. The spear-cat skull that protected his face fell away with a clatter.

He glared down into wide indigo eyes, feeling a jolt of shock as he did so.

You!

She was trying to pry his fingers from around her throat as she fought for the breath his grip denied her. Khalvir gritted his teeth and tightened his hold, knowing that if she spoke, she would place him back under her spell.

He couldn't believe this turn of fortune. His elusive quarry had come to *him,* come to meet her fate. The need for revenge seared above all others, burning away any other thought. Revenge for what she had done, revenge for what that other witch had done. Reaching back quickly, Khalvir drew his knife and placed the blade against her throat. She would never cast another spell.

In that instant, she found the strength to pull his fingers a fraction away from her throat. Enough to get the breath she needed to scream: "Juaan! No!"

It was as if someone had burned his hand. Burned his mind. Suddenly powerless, Khalvir fell back. His heart thudded inside his chest, flaming with an emotion he did not understand. Shocked, he pressed himself against the rock wall of his prison. Only now did he notice he was at the bottom of a deep hole, with sheer rock rising all around him.

He stared across at the being who had bewitched him again. It was like he was looking at her with two separate pairs of eyes. To one, she was the most precious thing in the world to him. To the other, the most hated. Both perceptions warred against the other. Khalvir fought desperately to take back control of his mind. To break the witch's spell.

She was coming towards him, stumbling along with her arm outstretched. Her eyes burned with fervent joy. "Juaan. My Juaan," she repeated over and over. Each word caused his heart to stutter and leap inside his chest. The call to answer her was almost too strong to resist.

He *had* to resist this trickery. As she drew closer, Khalvir raised his blade. He could not let her come any nearer.

Pain flickered over her face at his threatening gesture. She stared at him, askance. "Juaan, it's me," she appealed. "It's Nyri."

Another stutter. His head swam. He felt like he should know something, something very important, but the answer danced just out of his reach.

No! This was elf mischief! She was trying to rob him of his senses so that he would be helpless before her.

"My name is Khalvir," he hissed from between his teeth, fighting against her hold. "If you dare to come near me again, I *will* kill you."

A powerful wave of despair rolled through him at those words, but he fought it down, keeping his hand steady upon his weapon.

"Juaan. It's Nyriaana." She repeated, the hurt now plain in her eyes. "Don't you know me?"

Don't you know me...

Khalvir almost dropped his knife to put his hands against his aching head. It felt like it would explode. *Nyriaana. Don't you know me?* Her voice echoed around and around his mind, and he felt something he hadn't felt in a long time: terror.

She was trying to approach again. He mastered his fear as he had been taught and tightened his grip on his knife.

"Keep away, she-elf," he gritted between his teeth.

She was still approaching. Panic ripped through him as the hand holding his weapon refused to obey his commands. He could not strike, not even to save his life. It made him miscalculate. As he stepped to the side to put more distance between himself and the witch, he shifted his full weight upon his broken leg.

Agony ripped through him, lancing all up and down his back, robbing him of breath. His vision hazed. He tried to fight, but he was weak and he had nothing more to give. Khalvir's vision turned black. The last thing he remembered was her voice crying out: "Juaan!"

He fell to the ground senseless. For the first time in his life, Khalvir was at his enemy's mercy.

***

CHAPTER 3

A LEADER LOST

Galahir paced the edges of the elf forest, throwing glances into the shadows.

I will return when I have finished with her. Wait for me on the borders.

Galahir had waited. Three times the great glowing orb of Utu had passed overhead, and there was still no sign of Khalvir's return. Galahir ran a hand through his mane of tangled, sandy coloured hair. *Why* had Khalvir gone back to the witches? It was more than the need to appease their Chief. There had been a strange light in his friend's eyes that Galahir had never seen before. It had unnerved him. He hadn't wanted to let Khalvir go, but he was bound to obey him as his leader.

To Ea with orders! Now Khalvir was missing because Galahir had gone against his instincts.

"You couldn't have stopped him, Galahir," Banahir spoke from where he crouched beside the campfire they had made. "Do not blame yourself for his choice."

Galahir blew out a breath through his nose and continued to peer into the shadows between the trees. *Come on, Khalvir...*

"He's dead, Galahir," Lorhir snorted beside Banahir. "Those wolves would have got him, just like they did them." He jabbed his thumb towards the pile of five mutilated bodies lying away on the frosty plain; fallen brothers they had dragged from the woods once the wolves had given up on the chase.

Galahir pressed his lips together at the sight of them.

"Lingering here is a waste, of time," Lorhir went on. "He is lost."

"No, he is not!" Galahir snapped, his temper rising at Lorhir's gloating tone. No one could get under his skin like Lorhir could. "He knew what he was doing. He is the best warrior in the clan besides the Chief," Galahir hit back. "If anyone can survive in there, *he* can."

Galahir turned away from Lorhir's pitying gaze. Khalvir was *not* lost. That was just wishful thinking on Lorhir's part. The gods could not be that cruel. *They can*, his betraying mind murmured. *You know all too well what they let happen to your mate and child...*

"And so we're just going to sit here on the borders of this haunted forest and wait for his return?" Lorhir's tone made his opinion of Galahir's intellect clear.

"*We* are." Galahir shifted back to the fire and indicated the remaining warriors sitting in its glow. "Khalvir's last order was for *you* to report back to the Chief and then to return with further orders."

He had the satisfaction of seeing Lorhir's mouth fall open in consternation. "But that will take days!"

Galahir smiled tightly. "That is what Khalvir wished."

"Khalvir is *dead*, you half-Thal fool!" Lorhir spat and Galahir felt the colour rise in his cheeks at the insult. "Who left you in charge?"

"Khalvir." Galahir responded.

Lorhir barked out a laugh. "You are not fit to lead the women on a morning forage. *I* say we should leave this place and return to the camp. There is no telling when those wolves might decide to return to finish what they started."

Galahir set his feet. "No."

Despite his show of strength, his heart was pounding in his chest. He had never dared to take a stand before, but he knew if he didn't secure leadership now, Khalvir would be lost.

Lorhir leaped from the side of the fire, spear in hand. "I don't give a pile of horse dung what you think, Galahir! You—"

Then Banahir was at Galahir's side. "There are elves in those woods, Lorhir," he reasoned. "Are *you* going to be the one to tell the Chief that we turned and ran when the most coveted prize was within our grasp?"

Lorhir paled. Galahir was surprised but grateful for Banahir's support. He knew the other man had no real loyalty to him, but no one liked the idea of Lorhir in a position of power.

Lorhir let his spear fall to his side as several others joined Banahir at Galahir's side. His dark eyes glinted maliciously at Galahir. "Looks like someone has saved your pale hide once again," he drawled. "But once I tell the Chief of what happened here, you had better pray to the gods for mercy."

The gods have none. Boosted by the support of the other men, Galahir held his ground. Maddened, Lorhir spat at him before gathering his weapons and a share of the spoils from the elven settlement. Without a backward glance, he set off across the plain.

Galahir knew it was wrong to wish ill upon a brother in arms, but he hoped a spear cat got him before he ever reached his destination.

"My thanks," he muttered to Banahir.

The other man shrugged and returned to the campfire. "What *are* our plans, then?" he asked.

Galahir turned the situation over in his head. In sending Lorhir as Khalvir had wished, he had brought himself more time. He *had* to find Khalvir and learn his friend's fate before Lorhir returned, whatever that fate may be. He owed it to him.

"Those of us who are not wounded will make a pyre for the dead. There are too many to take back to camp and we cannot risk attracting predators."

"We're going to burn them?" Ranab, Banahir's younger brother's tone was askance.

"Yes," Galahir replied. For a moment, looking into their unfriendly gazes, he wavered. *What would Khalvir do?* Galahir straightened his back. "Unless you have the strength to waste on trying to break this ground?"

Ranab fell silent, and Galahir felt a thrill of victory. They thought he didn't learn, but he did. Slowly. "Those who are injured will have time to recover. The rest of us will go back into the forest and search for Khalvir."

"You want to go back into that forest and provoke the elves again?" Banahir's brows shot towards his hairline. Galahir could see the other man was already regretting his decision taking Galahir's side against Lorhir. "You realise those wolves already destroyed half of our group, don't you?"

"Yes." Galahir sighed. He wasn't *that* simple. "We will be take care not to provoke the elves. We will enter the forest in small numbers and make a search. If they are holding Khalvir captive, then we owe it to our brother to free him. We *cannot* leave him to the mercy of our enemies. You know what elves do to ones such as him."

"And what if he is already dead?"

Galahir frowned, thinking hard. *He* would risk his life to learn the fate of his friend, even if that fate turned out to be death. The others, however, were another matter. "Then... at least we will gain knowledge of the elves' strengths and weaknesses. When Lorhir returns, we will be prepared to carry out our Chief's commands."

This logic appeared to satisfy the rest of his company. Pleasing the Chief and avoiding his wrath was the one thing they all desired. No one crossed the Chief.

Galahir pushed down the familiar stirrings of fear at the thought of the Chief and returned to his vigil of the forest. *Hold on, my friend,* he thought. *I'm coming for you.*

***

Chapter 4

RESISTANCE

When Khalvir awoke again, it was dark. He blinked against the pressing blackness, his warrior instincts driving him to orientate himself as quickly as possible. For a moment, he remained still. The forest's night voice buzzed all around. Chirrups, hums, croaks. And nothing else. No other breath, no shift of weight. He was alone. The elf had gone. Cautiously, he sat up.

Khalvir couldn't even be sure now that she had been real. Now that he was more alert, he wondered if he had not imagined the entire nightmare; drunk on pain as he had been. He remembered collapsing in front of her, an enemy who would see him dead for no other reason than his mixed blood. And here he was; still alive. That was all the confirmation Khalvir needed to pass her off as a figment of his imagination.

What a hallucination to have! He remembered her eyes, how powerless he had been before them, how everything inside had screamed at him not to harm her, that if he did, his own life would mean nothing. He shuddered at the thought of his enemy having that much power over him.

Khalvir tested his body. He felt only the mildest of pains in his side and in his leg. The broken bones must have been part of the nightmare, he noted with relief. He still felt weak, however. His stomach ached. Khalvir did not know how long it had been since he had last eaten. He needed food and water, and he needed them soon. Without them, he knew he had only days to live.

He reached out an arm and his fingers met stone. His heart sank. That part of his dream had at least been true. He was at the bottom of a rocky pit but, with the blackness of night pressing on his eyes, there was not much he could make out. Khalvir noticed with a thrill that he could not see the sky. There were no stars, no bright silver spirit of Nanna, only darkness.

He clenched his fist against the unease trickling through him. He was a man raised on open plains. Being trapped in here was the worst kind of torment. He had to get out. He had to find food and water.

Khalvir studied the walls within reach with his hands, running his fingers along the stone. They were smooth and rose well above his head.

Khalvir ground his teeth together. He must try to alert Galahir somehow. Gathering his breath, he blew a sharp, thrilling whistle to the air. It would sound like a bird call to any who heard it but, if his men were anywhere within range, they would understand it for the signal that it was and come for him. He listened raptly for a few moments, but there was no return call. He would have to wait.

Khalvir looked down to the little bag he kept tied to his waist, recalling in his dream how the elf had touched it and roused him from his sleep. He didn't know why he kept the thing, or why it roused such powerful feelings in him. Lorhir had tried to take it from him once, taunting him with it, for his attachment to an object that was clearly elven in make. That day, Lorhir had not remained standing and his defeat at Khalvir's hands had attracted the attention of the Chief. His *raknari* training had begun in earnest.

Khalvir tore his gaze away from the little bag and wrapped his arms around his legs. His fingers came up against something smooth and fleshy, not the texture of fur that he had been expecting. Khalvir froze and looked down. He could just make out that his leg was bound with tough leaves and fibres stripped from bark.

He flinched back just as the sound of leaves and branches being shifted above his head grated across his ears. He hissed a breath and made an automatic move for his knife.

It was gone.

He was defenceless, and his enemies had found him. Khalvir coiled, waiting for the elves to strike. Armed or not, he would not make it easy for them.

A single face appeared in the gap that had been made in the hole's coverings, along with a flood of pre-dawn light. Khalvir blinked and then rocked back.

It was *her*.

Her skin was flushed from exertion, her eyes bright with excitement. Her eyes... That feeling of helpless familiarity floored Khalvir again.

It hadn't been a dream.

He pressed his back against the rock wall, absorbing that realisation, struggling to understand her reasons for leaving him alive. He could not make sense of it, but he would not make the same mistake twice and fall so shamelessly into her thrall. Keeping his lips pressed together, he glared up at his captor as she gazed down upon him. He was glad when he saw her quail.

"H-hello," her light voice caught in her throat. She was intimidated. Good. Perhaps that would be enough to prevent her from coming down again and strengthening her hold. Indeed, she made no move to come closer. "Um. I-I brought you some food. Are you hungry?"

Her words caught him off guard, and his empty stomach burned in response, but Khalvir kept his reaction from his face. It was a trap, and he would not let her see his need. He must keep his wits about him until he discovered what her plan was, then exploit it in any way he could.

He looked around now that he could see more clearly. The pit that trapped him was four body lengths in diameter and roughly three body lengths high. The walls curved inwards, the edges of the mouth crouching threateningly over him. There was little chance of climbing out, he noted in frustration.

"Here." He was in time to see her pull a large yellow fruit into view. "This is sweet. Try it." The elf threw the round fruit into the pit. In his peripheral vision, Khalvir watched it fall, bounce once on the hard ground, then roll away. He knew where it had come to rest, but he made no move to pick it up. He kept his eyes only on her.

He would not eat a thing she brought him. It made no sense for her to feed him, other than to poison him, or worse. Who knew what she might have coated on that fruit to dull and confuse his senses.

Disappointment flickered over her shadowed features. She sat down on the edge of the pit and produced a huge nut that was half the size of her own head. Cracking it down the seam in the middle, she picked at the firm, creamy contents.

Khalvir's traitorous stomach growled. Before he could stop himself, his eyes had flickered to the golden fruit she had tossed down to him. He berated himself for the lapse and glared up at the she-elf above. She was still eating slowly, deliberately. Taunting him. His anger burned hotter. He would not be baited like an animal in a pit. He lifted his chin in defiance.

He heard her sigh. How was it that the sound was somehow more familiar to him than his own breath?

"I healed your wounds. You were badly hurt from your fall," she said in her soft, coaxing voice.

Khalvir remembered his leg with a cold thrill. He had never believed in the healing powers of the elves, powers that his Chief so craved to possess. Now he believed it and the realisation came too late. The power this tiny girl must possess was nothing he had ever dreamt possible, and he was her prisoner, trapped and without defence.

"It's all right, Juaan. It will heal. I would never do anything to harm you."

Juaan. Explosions went off in his mind. Flashes of colour, ghosts of scent and sensation all danced just out of reach. They threatened to overwhelm him, but Khalvir could make no sense of them. He could see nothing clearly. He fought to clear his mind. *Stop!* He wanted to scream at the elf above. *She* was doing this. With a supreme effort, he kept his gaze steady, angrily defying her trickery.

It seemed to work. The she-elf fell silent, her mouth turning down. He felt a thrill of victory at the sight, but somehow it was marred by the inexplicable need to reach out and comfort her. The same need made him want to pick up that fruit and eat it, just to take that look of sadness off her face but, at the same time, a deeper instinct told him it would take more than eating a fruit to remove such a look. He almost growled, furious. He could no longer trust his own reactions!

As he struggled with himself, the she-elf got to her feet, the leaves she wore rustling as softly as those in the trees above. She fussed around the edges of the pit. Khalvir tried not to admire the grace with which she moved. So soft and delicate. The strange protectiveness he felt rose, unbidden, and he quashed it ruthlessly as she began stripping a vine from the side of a tree rising at the edge of the pit.

As soon as she had a reasonable length, she turned and threw the vine over the lip. It dangled just above the ground near to where Khalvir sat. Shock and relief rippled through him. *The fool!* She had just given him a means to escape.

His intent must have shown in his eyes. "It won't hold your weight," she warned. "It supplies water. Here." She cast down an empty nutshell half of the same kind she had just been eating from.

With his rising hopes of escaping this awful hole dashed, Khalvir snarled, and she shrank back. The red-gold shade of her skin was becoming more clear. Utu was rising somewhere behind the thick canopy overhead.

"I have to go." Despite her obvious misgivings, her voice was reluctant. "But I will return when I can with more food. Take this for now." She threw down the remains of her half-eaten nut. "It's going to be hard for me to come here often, but I will come back. Trust me."

Trust you? Khalvir raised an eyebrow. She was very naïve. And young. That strange need to protect her rose once more against his will.

A faint smile touched her lips at the expression on his face. She appeared to have won something from him, though he could not guess what.

"You will remember me, Juaan. I promise."

The flashes went off in his head. *No!* He pushed them back, hatred flaring as she turned and disappeared from sight.

CHAPTER 5

FURY

K halvir sat staring at the fruit. With each moment that passed, it seemed to grow in his vision. His stomach clawed inside his belly like a ravening beast. The golden globe became his enemy. An enemy that must be overcome. The only opponent he had ever lost to was his Chief. He wasn't about to be defeated now by a piece of fruit.

His leg wasn't yet strong enough to allow him to walk, and Khalvir felt sore and irritable. His thirst burned in his throat. He had been forced to try the vine she had provided as his vision hazed from deprivation. But he was only able to suck the barest amount of moisture from the strange funnels protruding from the sides. Not enough. His only hope was for his men to return for him.

He had ordered Galahir to wait, but he knew his friend would disobey and search for him eventually. Galahir was loyal to a fault. Khalvir weighed his chances of being found. This forest was vast and he was well hidden.

Of his own free will, Galahir would continue until all hope of Khalvir being found alive was lost. But the choice may not be his when he had the other men and the Chief's orders to consider. Lorhir would insist on leaving.

With Khalvir out of the way, the Chief would most likely place Lorhir as leader of the *raknari*. A position the wily jackal had coveted for many, many passing summers. It would not take him long to try to convince the others that searching for Khalvir was a lost cause.

The golden globe of fruit interrupted his thoughts, breaking in on his concentration. Khalvir glared at it in open defiance. It stared back, impressively unmoved. It seemed to know it would eventually win.

Khalvir groaned. He was doing battle with a fruit. He looked again at the offending object, asking himself if it was wise not to eat. Perhaps he should take it. If the opportunity came to escape, he needed the strength to stand, to run.

The fruit gazed on smugly.

Khalvir hissed, laying his head on his arms as they locked around his knees so he was facing in the opposite direction. He stared instead at the blank rock wall. At least that didn't look appetising. He traced shapes in the rocks to pass the time until darkness crept back into the pit. He tried to sleep as a way to escape his hunger, but his leg ached with the pangs of healing and the unyielding ground offered no comfort. He slept in fits and snatches. The forest was too loud. He missed the near silence of the open plains. Did elves sleep at all in this din?

When Khalvir did find sleep, indigo eyes stared back at him behind his lids, taunting him with the quiet secret that lay within their depths. A secret only she could know. Khalvir jerked upright, dispelling the vision. He clenched his teeth together and gave up on the idea of sleep. He was trapped in a pit of Ea's damnation. He supposed he had committed enough sin in his life to deserve it.

Khalvir felt rather than saw the night passing. The claustrophobia crawled over him, growing stronger with every moment as his own strength waned. His skin crawled at the confinement. He was finding it harder to remain upright. His whistling signals continued to go unanswered.

Just as Khalvir thought he could take it no longer and would throw himself at the rocks in an effort to break loose, the leaves above his prison shifted.

She had returned.

It alarmed Khalvir when it took several attempts to focus his eyes. Grey spots danced before his vision. He straightened his back and arranged his features into a semblance of hostility.

"I came back," she said breathlessly.

He kept his posture defensive, warning her away. He did not want her; he did not need her. She was unwelcome and if he could ever catch her, he would do what he came here to do and kill her in vengeance for his lost men.

He could not know when her nicety might run out and she would try to be rid of the abomination in her forest. The reason she had not already done so still eluded him, and an enemy whose purpose could not be understood was a deadly one.

"How are your injuries? Are you in any pain?"

Khalvir tightened his grip around his leg as she blatantly reminded him of her power. If she thought she could intimidate him, she was sorely mistaken.

Her face twisted into a plea. The expression grabbed at his heart, startling him. "Please," she begged, "try to remember. It's me. It's your Nyri."

Khalvir was quick to strangle the snatches of sensation that fired in his brain. Why was she torturing him like this? *Witch! Just leave me alone!* He clenched his fists in an attempt to control his rage. He saw her body tilt as if she were fighting not to take a step back from the look on his face.

The elf dropped her eyes, shifting her bare feet. "Aren't you going to eat?"

No! Can't you understand? He thought at her. *I will not give in to you.*

She dug her nails into her palms as she turned the full force of her eyes upon him. "Please, eat. *Please,*" she appealed. "You are dying. You cannot go on like this. Please."

He snorted. But then she reached out with one trembling hand.

"Please." Her voice cut through him like a knife. "What can I say? What can I do to prove myself to you? I do not mean you harm. Please, let me help, I need to be able to help *someone*—" Tears slipped silently down her cheeks.

Khalvir could no longer keep the carefully arranged hostility upon his face. The sight of her upset wreaked havoc in his heart. He raised his eyebrows in alarm. She was crying for him. She was crying for her *enemy*. He could not understand this girl. He could not understand his own reactions to her. He quite suddenly wanted to take her in his arms. Before he knew what he was doing, he leaned towards her.

No, no, no! He closed his eyes so that he could no longer see her face and tipped his head back against the rock wall. He was so exhausted, so tired. His will to resist her was crumbling with every moment. He *had* to resist. It was easier when he couldn't see her.

Khalvir heard her sniff back her tears.

"My tribe has posted extra watch," she said after a while, her voice having regained a measure of calm. Khalvir kept his eyes closed, trying to ignore how her voice flowed like a balm to his soul. "It is very important that you do not draw attention to yourself. Do you hear me?"

Khalvir couldn't help but open his eyes a crack to regard her. The more she spoke, the more of an enigma she became.

Hope sprang in her face and she pulled forth yet another enemy for him to contend with. A bunch of roots. "Maybe you'd prefer these." She coaxed. "Try them. Please."

Why was he even resisting any more? It seemed foolish now. A fault of pride. If she wanted to hurt him, surely she would have done it by now. He was so hungry…

"Juaan—"

Pain swept through him, followed swiftly by a wave of fury. The witch was still trying to cast her spell, and he had very nearly succumbed. She had weakened him to the point where he had almost been willing to give in, lulling him with her guile.

Anger such as he rarely let himself feel ripped through Khalvir's body. For the first time in a long time, he felt the unwanted beast within uncoiling. He was dimly aware of the colour draining from her face at the sight of his reaction.

"Get away from here, witch!" he hissed, his disused voice cracking and snarling through his teeth. She froze on the brink of the pit like a frightened deer before the hunter. It only angered him more. The hated energy in his chest that he longed to be rid of tore against his control like a wild beast. It was *all* her fault. He shot to his feet. "Get. *Away!*"

He could not get to her. He wanted to get to her, to break this dreadful spell. Desperate, Khalvir cast around. Spying a fist sized rock by his feet, he grabbed it and drew back his arm, fully prepared to throw. He could kill her so easily. He could see the points on her skull where the rock would crack bone and drop her senseless to the ground.

He gated a helpless wail of pain between his teeth as he imagined this and altered the angle of his hand just as he let fly the rock.

It grazed against her ear and bounced off the nearest tree with a resounding crack. She would never know that he had deliberately missed, nor how close she had come.

"Get away from here!" he snarled, injecting as much menace into his voice as he could. "Don't come back! Elf *witch*. I will kill you!"

He saw the moment her heart broke in her eyes, and it was one of the most terrible things he had ever witnessed. With tears of betrayal standing in her eyes, the elf turned from him and fled.

The energy within faded, curling back into his chest like a tamed spear cat. He had won. She would never come back. His anger gave way to despair and his knees buckled, his strength giving out at last.

Another wave of dizziness sent him to the ground. His body was shutting down. He was dying. As Khalvir faded towards darkness, he experienced the strangest sense of regret.

He would never see her face again

***

Chapter 6

SEARCH

Darkness was falling. Galahir clutched the wooden haft of his *arshu* in his right hand, feeling its reassuring weight as he twisted it at his side. The wind whistled through the sharpened stag's antlers, curving from each end. The weapon of a raknari warrior. It took seasons of practice to master. Galahir wondered if it would be enough to protect them now.

Not that he would voice this concern to Banahir, who stood edgily at his side, his own weapon in hand. Together, they faced the forest. Khalvir had not returned. It was time to make their first foray in their search for him.

Without a word, Galahir jammed the concealing ox skull over his head and started into the trees. He heard Banahir draw a breath and then follow, his own face protected by white bone.

Darkness pressed down upon Galahir's eyes as the cloying air of the woods filled his nostrils. He disliked hunting in forests.

"Where do we even begin?" Banahir gestured to the expanse of trees.

Galahir pressed his lips together. The forest was a big place. Even if the entire clan was here, it might still take them two turns of Nanna to search the whole area. Everything looked the same in the blackness. He wasn't even sure of the direction back to the elf settlement. But that did not mean he was about to give up.

Galahir slung his *arshu* across his shoulders. "We need to find the settlement again. If they're holding Khalvir, he is most likely to be there."

Banahir emitted a wordless hiss. Even beneath the skull that he wore, Galahir knew Banahir was not happy to be going near the elven settlement. Not without twenty other men at their backs. But the other man dipped his head in agreement, nevertheless.

Galahir struck out in the direction he believed they had initially taken when they had first found the abandoned settlement.

The leaves of the black canopy shifted restlessly overhead as Galahir and Banahir cut a path through the undergrowth, weaving through the trees. Night creatures croaked and whistled in a ceaseless din. If the wolves were approaching, they would not have a hope of hearing them until it was too late. Galahir kept his back against Banahir's as they circled around, weapons at the ready, straining to see into the oppressive blackness.

All light from the edge of the forest had been lost when Galahir pushed back the ox skull, enabling himself to raise his fingers to his lips and give one long, thrilling whistle.

"Shhh!" Banahir protested as the piercing sound shivered into nothingness. "Are you mad?"

"How else are we going to find him?" Galahir asked.

"I don't know, but just keep it down. Do you want to bring the witches down on our heads?"

"They won't know what it is they're hearing." Galahir dismissed.

Banahir grunted. "I don't like it. We are being watched. I *know* we are."

So did Galahir. He could not say how he knew, but he did. The way the hairs stirred on the back of his neck, sending a shiver down his spine. Even the trees appeared to scrutinise them.

Galahir pushed the sensation away as he listened for a returning call, but no answering whistle came back. He sighed. They needed to travel further in.

"Are you sure we're going in the right direction, Galahir?"

"No." Galahir paused and scanned the surrounding landscape. His eyes were adjusting to the gloom. The trees were grey sentinels in the darkness, pressing in on all sides. Galahir risked another whistle.

Nothing.

"We still have a long time until dawn," he said. "Let's keep to this direction and see if we come up against a landmark that will tell us we're getting close. We need to find that settlement again quickly if the Chief orders another raid."

"The Chief can hunt the elves down *himself* if he wants them so badly," Banahir whispered tersely. Speaking ill of their Chief in front of another indicated just how nervous the other man was. Galahir pretended not to have heard as they travelled on.

"Did you hear that?" Banahir hissed suddenly, breaking a lengthy silence.

"What?"

"Voices."

Galahir strained his ears over the incessant sounds of the forest. For a moment he heard nothing, then—

"*Ninmah's Mercy!*"

The sound was nothing more than a whisper in the air, easily mistaken for a rustling in the leaves. Galahir hunkered down into the undergrowth in front of a tree as Banahir did the same.

"*Kyaati!*"

Distant voices were raised in panic, as soft as the breeze. Galahir could not tell the direction, only that they came from a long way off. He turned to Banahir, who had crouched behind him. "Perhaps—"

Galahir's words choked off in his throat as his eyes bulged.

"*What*?" Banahir's shoulders tensed.

"Don't. Move."

The massive spider was crawling down the tree towards Banahir's unsuspecting back. Galahir judged that if the creature had been on the ground, it would have reached the height of his knee. It travelled in fits and jerks, assessing the man who rested at the base of its lair. Banahir turned his head.

"Ea preserve us!" he cried out in shock as he leaped away from the tree, causing roosting birds to take flight overhead.

It was a mistake.

Provoked by the sudden movement, the spider lunged. Quick as a striking snake, it leaped at Banahir, fangs as long as a finger extending towards the enemy in its sights. In his haste to escape, Banahir stumbled over a tree root and collapsed into the undergrowth.

Galahir reacted before he was conscious of doing so. Even as the spider leaped, he was bringing his *arshu* to bear. One end of the antler tipped weapon caught the arachnid in mid air, puncturing its body and flinging it away into the undergrowth. Its shrieks of surprise and pain ripped through the surrounding forest.

Galahir grabbed Banahir's arm and yanked him back to his feet. The forest was rustling all around them, agitated by the spider's continued shrieking.

"Time to go," Galahir panted, his heart sinking. Their cover was blown. Witches or wolves could already be converging on their position. Banahir at his side, Galahir sprinted back along the path they had created, back towards the safety of the plains.

I'm sorry, Khalvir.

Tonight would not be the night he found his friend, but Galahir vowed he would return. Monster spiders be damned. He would search this forest every night until he discovered what had become of Khalvir.

***

CHAPTER 7

DEFEAT

There were whispers, whispers in the darkness of his mind. Khalvir hazed in and out of consciousness, unsure if he was dreaming or awake. He thought he heard the leaves above him move once, and a triumphant laugh grazed across his ears. It was not *her* laugh. This laugh was ancient, like the sound of dry leaves crackling.

"I knew it. So, you have come back, boy," the voice whispered in the shadows of his mind. "The Great Spirit does indeed work in mysterious ways."

He drifted. The next thing he heard was the whisper of many feet and voices tense with panic.

"Ninmah's Mercy!" a male voice cried in the far distance.

Khalvir tried to rouse himself. There was danger. He had to get up, but he could not feel his limbs, could not even open his eyes. The blackness sucked him back under completely.

The first thing he was aware of was water flowing over his lips. The sweet, cool flow was a relief against the cracked and parched flesh. Without thinking, he sipped it in, taking one swallow, then another.

Strength trickled through his veins and then became a river. And with that strength came awareness.

Khalvir somehow knew she was there before his physical senses were even aware of it. He had been wrong in thinking he would never see her again. She had returned and *dared* to re-enter the pit, even after all he had done.

Witch! He lashed out with an arm. His reactions were slower than normal, and he missed, barely brushing her shoulder with his fingertips as she skipped back. The weakness infuriated him.

He rolled up and promptly doubled over, the pain of healing bones and deprivation cutting through him.

"Careful," she murmured. "You won't have fully healed yet."

Khalvir glowered at her as he propped himself into a sitting position. The jabbing pain in his side almost had him doubling up again.

"Juaan." She had been standing poised by a dangling root, but at the sight of his discomfort, she took a step back towards him. Concern pinched her brow as one hand reached out. "Are—,"

You are *insane!* Shutting out the agony, Khalvir threw himself to his feet. He could take no more. His mind was so hazy, he no longer knew what was right. "I warned you!"

Ignoring the scream in his soul, he charged at her, fully intent on ending the witch once and for all. He would rather die than be her prisoner for a moment longer.

She stood, watching him come without so much twitching a finger. But then the indigo eyes ignited. Khalvir remembered that fire. It was the same fire that had confronted him at the base of the tree as she had defended her friend against him. The power of her fury was staggering.

"Kill me then!" she screamed up into his face. "Go on! Be rid of me!"

Her eyes burned him, her words singing his fury to ash. Desperately, Khalvir tried to cling on. He reached out a hand, intent on closing it around her throat and ending her torment. He was so tired. So tired.

His fingers refused to close, and she stepped boldly into his grasp. Her soft skin brushed his fingertips, making him shudder. She raised her chin, exposing her throat.

"Go on," she hissed. "Free me from my bond. There is no other way."

Khalvir's resolve shattered before her strength. He had nothing left with which to fight. He could not do it. He could not…

His knees buckled, and he collapsed in a helpless heap at her feet. He had never been so vulnerable. She had taken everything that he was.

"What spell have you cast on me, she-elf?" His voice cracked traitorously. "Who *are* you?"

She had not moved as he had fallen. It seemed to take her a moment to find her voice. "I told you. I am Nyri."

The sound of her name cut at him. "And why do you insist on tormenting me like this?"

He spied a flash of hurt in her eyes at the accusation. "Please," she implored. "I do not mean to torment you. I only want you to recover."

He raised his head with an effort. Her wide eyes were guileless. He believed her, but he still could not figure out her reasoning, and that filled him with doubt. Everyone had a reason. He must find hers. "You are an elf. I am nothing more than an abomination in your eyes. I know that well enough."

"You're wrong!" Her voice burst with unexpected passion. "You are *everything* to me, Juaan!"

Anger rolled through him as he tried to control himself. "I told you before," he bit out with as much strength as he could manage. "My name is not Juaan. I do not know who you have mistaken me for. My name is—"

"Khalvir." She cut him off bitterly. "Yes, I know."

Well, then, he thought to himself, *stop it.* He glowered at her for a moment longer before his eyes caught sight of something over her shoulder. His heart leaped. The length of root that she must be using to get in and out of this prison was dangling invitingly behind her.

Khalvir assessed his chances. He was weak, his leg only half healed, but he knew he was still stronger than the she-elf - and she was the only thing that stood between him and freedom. He didn't have to hurt her, just get around her.

Unfortunately, she read the intent in his eyes. "Do not attempt to escape. I have a pack of wolves up there who do not take kindly to strangers in their territory. It took all of my skill to prevent them from coming down here to chew your head off. You wouldn't make it two strides."

For an instant her eyes grew distant, as if listening to some faraway sound that he could not hear. Khalvir was confused until a blistering cry ripped through the air above, echoing as it bounced off the walls of the pit. The hairs on Khalvir's arms bristled. It was the most menacing sound he knew. The howl of a wolf.

Khalvir clenched his teeth. How *dare* this tiny girl trifle with him. She had bound his warrior's instincts and now she had surrounded him with a pack of the blood-thirsty predators who had already killed many of his number. This witch was the most dangerous creature he had ever met.

She took a step back from the look on his face. "Are you going to hurt me?" Her voice was small, vulnerable, as if she were the one at his mercy and not the other way around.

The words went through him like the current from a bolt of lightning.

Are you going to hurt me?

Never.

The words flashed through his mind, spoken in a voice that was both unfamiliar and yet somehow central to him. He looked into her eyes and before he was really conscious of his own answer, he whispered: "No. I won't hurt you." Helplessness washed through him. "I can't, it seems. For the love of Ea, I do not know why."

Khalvir trembled like a defenceless child. Him, a survivor of countless battles and hardships, quivering before a girl.

A tentative smile was forming over her delicate face. She reached out a hand towards him. His fear spiked at the thought of her touch. Her words alone caused him enough torment. He could not bear to let her touch him as well. He knew instinctively that if she did that, he would fall completely under her spell and be forever lost.

She read the apprehension in his eyes and dropped her hand, a little frown of confusion marring the smooth skin between her slanting brows. "Don't worry," she murmured haltingly, as if she wasn't sure why she should have to say it. "I won't hurt you, either."

Khalvir nevertheless kept his eyes trained upon her as she lowered herself to squat a couple of paces away. He waited for her to say more, but she lapsed into silence and *stared* at him. Her indigo eyes scrutinised his face, seeming to miss nothing.

His annoyance rose as he fought the urge to squirm. She had won. Now here she was, rubbing her victory in his face by studying him like some strange creature she had found beneath a rock. Khalvir was accustomed to men being taken aback by his unusual appearance, by his half elf heritage, and he no longer let their reactions bother him. This was somehow more personal.

In the end, he could take it no longer. He hadn't intended to speak again, but he needed her to stop looking at him like that. "What?" he snapped.

His harsh question shook her from her deep reverie. "Sorry. I was just thinking, now that we have established we will not hurt one another, are you hungry?"

She would not give it up. The stubbornness Khalvir had clung to for days resurfaced. This was the one thing she hadn't yet taken from his control. Weak as he was, he was not prepared to surrender that last shred of his dignity. "No."

Her eyes were suddenly over bright with some inexplicable emotion. "Don't be stubborn."

You— Her audacity was shocking, and it took Khalvir a moment to form his own reply. "I'm not being stubborn!" he snapped at last. "Why should I trust you? It is in your best interest to kill me." *Why leave an enemy that could hurt you alive?*

"And it is in *your* best interest to kill me," she countered smoothly. "You could do so so easily. That first time I came here, you had me pinned to the ground and at your mercy. And again just now. You could have hurt me, killed me, but you didn't. You let me go. Why?"

She had him. Confusion clouded his mind. Why, indeed? She was his enemy, an enemy who held his very life in her hands. She was dangerous. Khalvir knew what he needed to do, what he *should* do to survive. He had been raised to survive. It wasn't as if he hadn't faced such a choice before; his enemy's life or his own. This girl should by now be another painful memory on top of a river of regrets. And yet here she sat, challenging him once again with those dreadful eyes. Eyes that reached right into his soul and utterly possessed him.

"I. Don't. Know." He ground each word from between his teeth in answer to her hated question. "By the Sky Gods, I have reason enough."

"Well, *I* know," she said. "And it is for the same reason I will never hurt you."

"Will you stop that," he began hotly, "I am not—"

"Look," she cut him off again, in complete control. "It doesn't matter who I might have mistaken you for or who you mistakenly think you are. You either trust me or you die. You are dying. I can feel it. I am offering you survival. The choice is yours."

Her audacity stunned him again as she neatly overcame his last shred of control. Survival was all. He had to survive. He had to live to protect his clan. He was no use to them dead. Khalvir needed to get back to them, and he could not do that as weak as he was. If he were stronger, perhaps he could resist the witch's wiles more easily. The cloying air of the forest curled around his mind like smoke.

"I have a surprise for you," she blurted and reached into the folds of her garments, her face now childlike with excitement.

Khalvir recoiled instinctively from whatever she had concealed. He did not know what to expect. He had to look twice before his blurring eyesight confirmed that she held nothing more threatening than a bunch of berries.

"What?" She rolled her eyes. "Did you think I was going to pull a snake out of there?"

He snorted. "Who knows with your kind."

"My kind?" Now there was a flash of anger in her eyes; he had struck a nerve. She was so easy to read in a lot of ways. Khalvir felt a thrill of victory at unbalancing her insufferable calm. "The Woves you brought here are worse than any snake!"

"Woves?" That was a new one.

"Yes. Woves," she snapped. "The murderous dark spirits who followed you here. By all rights, I should pull a snake on you. Now, do you want this fruit or not?"

Khalvir knew he must not smile. He must not. He struggled to control his features. The fierce posture of her little body as she held forth a bunch of berries was suddenly the most amusing sight he had seen in a long time. Once again, he couldn't help but admire her courage. "You are a spirited one."

"Do you want them or not?" There was a definite edge of petulance in her tone now.

Khalvir looked at the shiny red berries in her small, long-fingered hand. His mouth watered. For some reason, this fruit was harder to resist than anything she had offered so far. His last bastion of resistance crumbled. But he still wasn't about to allow her to get near.

"Alright, have it your way." He gave in to her. "But first, put them on the ground and move away."

"Why? I'm not going to bite you."

"That's the least of my worries. You have the audacity to call me a murderer? I know what you could do if you touched me."

"Like what exactly?"

"You tell me, elf-witch. If you indeed have the power to do this." He indicated his leg. "What else are you capable of?"

"Elf? Witch?" Her brow pinched together. "That's rather ungrateful. Would you rather I had left your leg snapped in two?"

He clenched his teeth together. "Even so. Move away."

"Oh, for Ninmah's sake!" She placed the berries on the ground and backed off.

Khalvir watched her move to a safe distance and then stared at the fruit. He could resist no longer. He descended on the berries. He tasted the first tentatively. The sweet juices exploded inside his parched mouth, quenching his terrible thirst and hunger all in one bite. This was surely one of the most delicious things he had ever tasted.

More of those odd, nagging flashes went off in his head, but Khalvir was too hungry to care. He wolfed down the rest of the berries. They were gone in moments. His tortured belly uncoiled. He looked around for more, but that seemed to be it for the red fruit.

The elf murmured something he didn't quite catch in his distracted state. She was sitting, chewing on one of those now familiar golden fruits, watching him. Only now did he notice how painfully drawn she looked. Eating seemed to be a relief for her, too. She couldn't possibly be starving as much as him, could she? Khalvir felt a shiver of concern for her before he quashed it.

She ate half of the fruit before laying the remains on the ground in offering. Scooping up the halved nutshell she had thrown down to him days before, she got to her feet and approached the delicate vine that she had claimed would provide him with water. Before he could tell her how mistaken she had been, the elf-witch laid her hand on the fleshy stem. Khalvir watched in amazement as water flowed freely from one of the strange funnels protruding from the length of the stem. She filled the nutshell half to the brim and then balanced it carefully on the ground, so as not to spill a drop.

"I need to go now before I'm missed."

Khalvir berated himself for the faint wave of disappointment her words caused him. There was something else that needed to be answered. A question that still bothered him deeply. "What is it you want from me?"

Her breath caught in her throat as she looked back into his eyes. Uncertainty flickered over her face as she started for the root that was her way out. "Nothing."

"Nothing? Well, just how long are you planning to keep me down here?"

"I don't know that, either. We'll just have to see what the future brings."

Khalvir tensed. That was no answer. His enemy did not know her own purpose for keeping him? He did not know how much longer he could stand being trapped in this pit. He felt like he was drowning in a nightmare, and she was the cause of it all. Frustration bubbled up inside him. "Has anyone ever told you that you are a little monster?"

Khalvir was alarmed when she laughed and cried at the same time.

"Yes." The witch smiled through her tears. "You. Several times."

Khalvir made his mind up. She *was* insane.

She pulled herself together. "I must go. Rest," she ordered. "You need to get your strength back. I'll return with more food, but I have to be careful. I cannot let my People become suspicious. They *would* let the wolves chew your head off."

So, the rest of her kind did not know of his presence. Khalvir's confusion deepened.

"Why?"

"Why what?"

"Are you protecting me from your own?"

She turned then, and the look in her eyes made Khalvir's heart catch in his chest, filled as they were with an abiding adoration and... love. No one had ever looked at him in such a way.

"Because... no matter what has happened or who you have become, you are still my Juaan and I will protect you to the end."

She was up the rope and gone before Khalvir could hope to formulate a response. Gone before his heart could return to a normal pace or understand how to feel about anything at all.

Chapter 8

Accepance

Days passed as Khalvir sat in the pit and tried not to think. He whistled to the forest and strained to hear any sort of response, waiting for Galahir to respond. His hope that they were searching for him waned. They must think him dead by now. The last time Galahir had seen him, he had been running recklessly into the jaws of the enemy.

At least all of his immediate enemies had been defeated. The pit was now devoid of food. He'd enjoyed most of what the witch had brought him, though none had appealed as much as those red berries.

The only offerings he could not bring himself to choke down were a couple of large, tough looking roots. The flavour was so bitter it was offensive. He tossed those out of the pit so the witch would not see the leftovers whenever she returned. She may well use her power over him and force him to eat them.

Try as he might, Khalvir could not stop himself from thinking and remembering the look on her face as she had vowed that she would protect him to the end. What bothered him the most was his own response. The feelings that had arisen in his heart as she looked at him in such a way disturbed him more deeply than he cared to admit.

He could not make sense of them, and he knew for certain that they should not exist.

She was an elf-witch and for that alone, he should hate her with all his being. Elves had tried to kill him as a boy. His own kin. His mother's family. They had stolen his childhood memories and tried to kill him for being who he was. A half-bred abomination.

Hate rose within at the thought. If it hadn't been for the intervention of his Chief and his clan, he would be dead. Khalvir had no memory of the event. He only remembered waking, dazed in the middle of an elf settlement. The elves had all been dead, apart from the women and children his clan had captured. The trees had been blackened and burned. Khalvir could still taste the smoke in the air.

His Chief was the first thing he remembered, huge and terrifying to the boy he had been. At first Khalvir had borne an irrational hate for the man, but he had soon come to see the truth of what the Chief told him. The elves hated him. Loathing had twisted the faces of the elf captives as they had travelled with his new clan. They had spat upon him whenever he had foolishly tried to help the weak, naming him a Forbidden abomination and that everything was his fault. Khalvir had never forgotten.

And then there had been *her*. Khalvir curled in on himself as the pain of the memory sliced through him. He rarely permitted himself to think about that witch and what she had done. Just because of—No. The elves would be his enemies until his dying breath.

And so Khalvir brooded. The days blurred together, dull and unchanging. Utu rose and fell in the sky. Khalvir wished he could see her bright face, have her clear light cut through the ever-growing confusion in his soul. The forest was dim and hazy beneath the suffocating canopy, warping his mind with its cloying atmosphere. It was becoming harder to separate reality from a dream.

Only the she-elf's visits broke the tedium, becoming the unwanted highlight of his current existence. Khalvir hated the fact he was becoming so reliant on her. For food and company. She spoke occasionally, but he refused to respond, hoping she would lose interest and go away. He tried to avoid the emotions she evoked, for they shook the basis of all the beliefs he clung to.

Nevertheless, Khalvir watched her. She was terribly young, barely out of her adolescence, he guessed, but her presence was soft and restful, unless otherwise provoked.

He still found her eyes to be the most fascinating feature. They were impossibly expressive and betrayed a lot of what was going on inside her mind, even though half of the time Khalvir wished they didn't. There was a sadness there. She had known loss. She had known hardship. She cared too much. He could see it in the haunted shadows that dappled the indigo depths. And... there was a growing fear inside them. The latter concerned him more than it should, and he couldn't help but wonder at it. What would happen to her if her People found out she was keeping him? Another unwanted emotion took hold inside Khalvir's heart. Fear. Fear for *her*.

After three days of inactivity, he could bear it no longer. He needed to do something, anything.

The she-elf sat across from him in her usual position. She was silent for once, having given up at last on trying to coax a conversation out of him. Her eyes were distant, the skin around them tight. She was brooding over something. The frown between her brows was becoming a permanent crease.

Khalvir realised in that instant that he missed the sound of her voice and he broke his long held silence.

"You're quiet today, elf." He kept his expression cool. He could not let her know how much he was depending on her presence.

Her gaze flickered his way. "I thought you did not like me talking," she murmured to the ground. "It's not as if you talk back much."

Huh. Khalvir shrugged and let her have the point, turning over the fruit she had brought carefully in his fingers. "I suppose if you have to be here, listening to you chatter breaks the tedium."

She lifted her head, her sombre expression lifting despite his best efforts to keep his words as aloof as possible. It occurred to Khalvir that maybe she was becoming just as dependent on him as he was on her, and maybe that was something he could take advantage of. He should not pass up this opportunity.

"Well, what do you want to talk about?" she asked.

"How many are in your tribe?"

"Fifteen," she answered, not thinking twice about volunteering this information to an enemy. She was far too trusting.

Shock rippled through Khalvir at the answer. "So few?"

Her temper flared. "Yes, thanks to the Woves. It is only by the grace of Ninmah that we survive at all."

Khalvir ignored her outburst. He was too distracted. Fifteen would not appease his Chief after all the long seasons of fruitless searching.

"Are there other tribes?" Perhaps he could salvage something from all of this.

"Not that we have found." She kept her eyes on the ground, hiding from him.

That wasn't good. Khalvir continued to turn the fruit over in his hands. He picked another subject.

"What would your tribe do if they found out you were coming here?"

The laugh that burst from her lips was bitter, the concealed terror in her eyes burning to the fore. He had been right in his suspicions. "That is something I try hard not to think about."

Will they kill you? Khalvir didn't ask aloud. Grief ripped through him at the very notion. He forced it away. "I am your enemy," he said. "The enemy you say threatens your People's very survival and yet here you are risking capture and probably death to keep me alive. A Forbidden abomination. *Why?*" He had asked himself this question a hundred times, but he was still no closer to an answer.

"I have told you why," she muttered to an uncaring rock.

Irritation and awe rippled through him at the knowledge that she would risk herself so for someone she once knew. Her loyalty must know no bounds. Khalvir sighed. "He must have been very dear to you, this boy you knew, for you to risk yourself in such a way."

She gazed at him. The pain in her eyes was almost more than he could bear. "Yes," she said. "He was."

"I am sorry you lost such a person." And he *was* sorry for her pain. He couldn't help it. But he had to make her see sense. He had to make her let him go. For both their sakes. He seized upon a new tactic. "Let me ask, would he have wanted you to risk yourself in such a way?"

She brushed quickly at the tears sliding down her face. "Probably not," she admitted. "But it is no less than he would have done for me if the situation was reversed so, what choice do I have? We promised to look after each other. I will not break that vow."

Khalvir shook his head in disbelief. "And this boy was like me?" He gestured to his clearly half-elven appearance.

Her eyes were enigmatic. They seemed to say that he wasn't seeing something that was clear before him. He took her silence as a confirmation. She had loved a creature like him. Again, Khalvir was both moved and infuriated by her. Moved because he couldn't imagine such love. Infuriated because she was yet again shaking everything he had ever believed in. "You... are not what I expected from an elf."

She gave a wan smile. "Probably not, but here I am, foolish as it may seem."

Khalvir felt the wall of hate that he had been fighting so hard to keep around his heart, crumble and fall away. It wasn't just her strange magic keeping him from killing her now. No matter how much he wanted to, he could not hate this elf.

He looked her straight in the eye as she frowned, letting her know how serious he was. "You should not be putting yourself at risk. You... I do not think you are someone who deserves death."

His words did nothing to sway her. "I can take care of myself," she replied. "I know what I am doing and it is the right thing to do."

It was hopeless. Khalvir growled low in the back of his throat.

She rose somewhat reluctantly to her feet, and Khalvir realised with a pang that her time was up. She had to go back to her People. "I promise to come back tomorrow," she said. "Please stay quiet and wait for me."

"Tomorrow. I'll be here."

He watched her leave and couldn't help feeling that she was taking a little piece of his now defenceless heart with her.

No, no, no. Khalvir buried his face in his knees and stared into the darkness of his self-made cave. He was slipping further and further under her spell.

He needed to get out of this pit, out of this accursed forest. If he could just breathe clear, fresh air again, his mind would be free and his sense of self would return. He longed to be rid of this confusion and these half remembered sensations. Raising his head, Khalvir whistled long and loudly into the stillness.

Relief coursed through him when he was rewarded with the faintest answer.

***

The distant whistle came like music to Galahir's ears. After all the interminable nights of searching and leaving the forest each dawn with an ever diminishing hope, at last a sign.

"Was that—?" Banahir queried at his side as he withdrew his fingers from his mouth.

"Yes," Galahir breathed. "That was Khalvir. He *answered* us." The exhaustion lifted from his shoulders.

His friend was alive!

CHAPTER 9

AT BAY

"Khalvir is alive." Galahir announced to the rest of the group as he and Banahir returned to camp.

Their faces showed varying levels of disbelief.

"He answered our signal. He is in the forest somewhere and is calling for us." If it had been up to Galahir, he would have charged back into the forest without resting and torn the entire area apart until he had freed Khalvir from whatever trap he had fallen into.

But the elves had been watching them ever more closely from their unseen perches. To stay any longer had risked a reaction. Galahir would be forced to abandon any further attempts to find Khalvir if the elves attacked. He had too few men to resist them. Much as he chaffed against it, he had to maintain the delicate standoff with the witches within.

"Where did the signal come from?" Ranab asked.

"It is hard to tell within the trees," Banahir answered his brother. "But we believe it came from the west. The elven settlement lies somewhere in that direction. If we can re-find it, we will be prepared for when Lorhir returns with the Chief's orders."

There were several nods of agreement and a distinct lift in spirits.

"We will mount another search tonight," Galahir said. It would be the worst kind of torture waiting out the day now that he knew his brother was out there calling for rescue, but he would have to suffer it.

Settling down by the campfire, Galahir helped himself to a share of the meats roasting over the fire, savouring the juices as they rolled over his tongue, satiating the hunger in his belly. It had been a long night in the forest. Banahir had already rolled up in his furs next to the flames, and the soft sound of his snoring soon filled the air.

Galahir yawned widely, noticing his own exhaustion for the first time since hearing Khalvir's answering whistle. Thus far, Galahir had run every mission into the forest, not trusting the others to search with the same zeal that he would. Catching some sleep now would not hurt, and he would need all of his wits for the coming night.

"Ranab," he gestured sleepily to the other man. "Take watch."

As Ranab took up position, watching towards the constant menace that was the elven forest, Galahir rolled up in his furs and was asleep almost before he laid his head upon his arm.

It felt like he had barely closed his eyes when hands were shaking him awake. "Huh...?" he inquired sleepily.

"Get up, Galahir," Banahir muttered. "It is almost time."

Galahir blinked his eyes open and saw that Utu was low in the sky. Dusk was falling fast over the rolling plains. He grunted as he hauled himself heavily to his feet.

The knowledge that tonight may well be the night that they rescued Khalvir chased the lingering grogginess from his mind. He disliked being in charge. Galahir wasn't blind to the others' opinion on his intellect, and it made him uncomfortable. Were it not for the need to get the men to help him in his search for Khalvir, he would gladly have stepped back and let someone else take over the moment his friend had been lost.

Galahir looked to the rest of the men and was not surprised when it was Banahir that joined him. Donning their concealing skulls, Galahir took point as they struck out into the trees.

"His signal came from that direction," Galahir pointed with the tip of his *arshu*.

Banahir dipped his head in agreement.

Galahir tilted his face back to study the tangled branches above, feeling the familiar tingle travel down his spine. "I wish to all the gods we could see them," he muttered under his breath. "I hate going against an enemy I cannot see."

"I doubt anyone would say they enjoyed such a thing," Banahir pointed out, keeping his weapon in a ready position.

Galahir grunted and strode off into the undergrowth. He gave a few hopeful whistles as he travelled, but this time, there was no answer.

"We're still too far out," Banahir said. "We have to travel further in. And *perhaps* it would be wiser to keep a lower profile tonight if we are hoping to get anywhere near the elven settlement."

Galahir ground his teeth together, but let the subtle chastisement pass. In silence, they carried on into the forest as the trees closed ever more firmly about them. The familiar sense of entrapment washed over Galahir, and he fought to keep the anxiety at bay. His breaths echoed hollowly inside the ox skull covering his head.

The boughs above groaned and sighed as the wind moved through them. Their whispers filled the air. Galahir found his breath catching with every movement, fully expecting to see an elf witch crawling through the canopy above him.

"Do you hear that?" Banahir breathed.

Galahir froze and strained his ears, but all he could hear were the squawks and screams of night creatures. "What?"

"Water. I can hear running water. Wasn't there a river close by the settlement when we stumbled across it the last time?"

"Yes," Galahir whispered. He listened again, and now that he knew what he was searching for, he heard it. The distant music of water running over pebbles. His heart leapt. "If we find that river, we can follow it until it brings us to the settlement."

"Agreed."

At last, a direction. Galahir crept on into the undergrowth, keeping his ears trained on the flowing water. It was getting easier to detect, and he increased his pace. If they were getting close to the settlement, then Khalvir *must* be close by. Galahir needed to let him know that rescue was at hand.

Sucking in a lungful of breath, he prepared to let out a long, thrilling whistle.

"*No*!" Banahir caught Galahir around the shoulders. It took a moment for Galahir to realise that the other man was trying to tug him to the ground.

"Wha—?"

"Get *down*!" Banahir continued to pull.

The undergrowth rustled ahead and Galahir threw himself onto his belly just as a threatening growl sounded from the direction of the disturbance.

"*Wolves.*" Banahir hissed as he lay on the ground beside Galahir.

The rustling grew louder, and Galahir ceased to breathe. Silently, he slipped his hand down to his fur boot and pulled forth his hunting blade. He would only use it if absolutely necessary. If the beast got off just one cry of alert, then it would all be over.

The disturbance in the leaves faded and then stopped altogether. The silence was somehow more ominous.

"Has it moved on?"

Galahir shrugged, a cold sweat beginning in his palm as he gripped at his knife.

"We can't stay here," Banahir whispered after long moments had passed. "We need to try a different route."

Galahir dipped his head in acknowledgement and beckoned for Banahir to follow him as he crawled through the undergrowth on his belly, moving away from where they had heard the wolf.

His arms were beginning to ache from the effort of pulling himself forward when Galahir paused and listened again. To his relief, there were no sounds of pursuit. The surrounding undergrowth was still and silent. "I think it's safe now," he said, and cautiously pushed himself back to his feet. "Do you still hear the water?"

"No." Banahir's voice was strangled. "But I see *them*."

The hairs rose on the back of Galahir's neck as he turned to face the direction in which Banahir was staring.

A row of eyes glowed from the dark.

The wolf pack was arrayed before them, the pinpricks of their pupils glinting red in the low light. Unnaturally still, they watched. They did not charge nor make a sound. They simply sat and stared, blinking slowly. Galahir fell back a step and as he did so the wolves cocked their heads. All at once, in perfect unison.

It was the most eerie sight Galahir had ever witnessed. Unlocking his muscles with an effort, he continued to back slowly away from the wall of eyes, Banahir at his side, not daring to turn his back as they retreated. His mouth was dry as bone.

It wasn't until the last pair of eyes had been lost from view between the trees that Galahir gave the command. "*Run.*"

Banahir did not need telling twice. Galahir pounded along in the other man's wake, straining his ears for any sign of pursuit from the wolves. There wasn't one.

The only thing he detected was the ghostly echo of laughter as he retreated once more through the trees.

***

CHAPTER 10

BUILDING TRUST

S he did not come back.

The next morning came and went. Every so often Khalvir caught himself staring hopefully into the sheltering leaves and branches, waiting for them to lift away and for her face to appear. But as the slanting light shifted direction, he knew she was not coming.

She had promised to return, and she had not. Khalvir knew he should feel relieved. The more he saw her, the greater his feeling of confusion grew. He could not afford to fall into the trap of caring for her more than he already did. His men were coming for him. He would soon be away from her hold on him and know his own heart once more.

Nevertheless, the disappointment stung, and he was angry. He should have known better than to trust an elf witch. Khalvir could not understand how he had so easily forgotten an entire lifetime of learning after just a few days of knowing her. This betrayal brought home just how much of a fool he had already been.

Furious, he paced around his prison like a cornered spear cat. But in the deepest recess of his heart, Khalvir knew it was not the sense of betrayal that made him fractious; it was the fear. She had not struck him as one who would break her word easily.

Something had happened.

Anxiety clutched at his heart at the thought of what could have befallen her. Perhaps she was dead, discovered by her People. A chill swept through him, and Khalvir sank stiffly to the ground. His limbs ached. He was exhausted. Sleeping on bare rock night after night was taking its toll. *Where* is *she?*

Hunger gnawed. The elf's offerings were hardly enough. Khalvir struggled to keep his thoughts from imagining hunks of sizzling meat straight from the campfire. But at least what she brought had been adequate to sustain him, to keep the terrible hunger at bay. Now she was gone, and he had nothing. He would not survive without her.

A fresh wave of annoyance at himself for having become so dependent on her visits swept through Khalvir. It had cost him. He should have been seeking ways to escape, not guiltily looking forward to the next time he would look into her eyes. He pushed away the crushing thought that he might never see them again. He could not entertain such thoughts now. He should not be having them, anyway.

Khalvir whistled hopefully, but there was no reply. After that first faint answer the previous night, he had heard no more. He feared he had imagined it, but, real or not, for now he was on his own. It was time to do what he should have done from the start. It was time to get out of this pit. Khalvir tested his muscles. He still hadn't returned to full strength, but it would have to be enough. Now the elf was gone. He was only going to grow weaker. It was now or never.

Khalvir studied the walls of his prison. They were not as smooth as they appeared at first glance. He was sure he could manage it. He listened, aware that it was not only this pit that ensnared him. He could hear nothing from above; only the usual sounds of the forest that never rested. A wolf pack had to leave to hunt sometime. He would just have to be careful that he did not end up being the target.

Determination hardening with every moment, Khalvir selected the most likely place for escape; the roughest part of the wall he could find. The foot and hand holds barely earned the title, but they would do.

His first attempt landed him back on the rock after he had climbed no higher than his own shoulder. That sequence of holds would get him nowhere. He moved to try a different route. Then another as that proved just as futile.

As Utu waned somewhere unseen, the fading light found Khalvir battered, bruised and close to exhaustion. Each attempt had pitched him hard to the waiting rock below. His leg screamed at the abuse. It was a testament to the she-elf's skill that it had not yet re-broken. He forced the thought of her from his mind. There was one more route left to try.

Khalvir clambered back to his feet. Setting his will and ignoring the pain of his body, he faced down his enemy, catching hold of the first handhold for the last time. He was careful, choosing only the tried and tested grips, no matter how far he had to stretch to reach them. Up he went. And up. His heart beat faster. This was higher than he had yet achieved. Up. His legs and arms shook from the effort of clinging with the barest tips of his fingers and toes. Khalvir gritted his teeth and fought on. Only the slight overhang could stop him now. Victory was in his grasp. He paused, gathering his remaining strength, then went forward.

His weight yanked him back, threatening to plunge him into the depths below. It was impossible. He was almost inverted with the ground when his hold failed. His stomach found his throat as he tumbled away into the darkness. He seemed to fall forever, though he knew in reality it only lasted for a few sickening heartbeats.

Khalvir crashed into the waiting rock, his right hand twisting beneath him. He felt it when the bones in his fingers shattered.

Stifling the scream that wanted to break past his lips, he panted against the pain and propped himself, one-handed, into a sitting position at the bottom of the rock wall. Wincing, he looked down at his crooked and now useless fingers. Agony ripped up and down his arm. He removed the hand from his hazing vision and put it gingerly on the cold rock, hoping to numb the sensation. The bitter tang of defeat washed over his tongue. There would be no escape for him. Not now.

This pit would be his tomb.

That was the last thought he had before unconsciousness pulled him under.

Something warm was touching his hand. He was freezing, and the warmth was soothing. Consciousness returned slowly. Everywhere hurt. Khalvir didn't think there was any part of his body that wasn't bruised. The sharp ache in his fingers shot up his arm as he twitched them unconsciously. The warmth tempered it.

Warmth.

He opened his eyes.

And she was there, like the magical being that she was, appearing and disappearing in the darkness. It felt like a dream and he drifted with it. She did not know that she was being watched. She was intent on his hand as she traced his rough skin with the delicate tips of her fingers.

Khalvir had never studied her face this close before. She was beautiful, he realised. Her large eyes that so captivated his soul were in turn as easy for him to read as a game trail and yet as mysterious as the Sacred Pools within the Mountains. The colour of them offset the pale red-gold shade of her smooth skin. The black waterfall of her hair tumbled over her slight shoulders.

Quite suddenly, Khalvir wanted to reach out and catch the stray strand that blew across her face, just to see if it was as soft as it looked. His tomb suddenly seemed that much brighter.

And that frightened him. The veil of the dream lifted.

"Don't."

The sound of his voice startled her. Khalvir felt a stab of loss as she dropped his hand. Released, he was quick to hide the broken fingers from sight.

"Don't what?" she asked breathlessly.

"Creep up on me. I don't like it. I could hurt you and I gave you my word that I would not." No one had ever crept up on him like she had just done while he slept.

"I'm sorry." She looked contrite. "I did not mean to." She nodded at the hand he had hidden from her, frowning. "What have you been doing?"

Khalvir felt the first stirrings of annoyance with her. Here she was, alive and well after making him think she was dead, after letting him think he would die here. Here she was once again stirring feelings in him he should not have. He should not let her get so close. He had vowed never to let her touch him.

Khalvir straightened his back, distancing her and his voice. When he answered, it was in a sharper tone than he intended. "What do you think? You don't expect me to just sit here, do you, waiting placidly for you to come back?"

"You tried to climb out? You can't climb out of this Pit. It's sheer rock!"

He tried to ignore the flash of hurt and betrayal that tightened her eyes. It was no less than what she had done to him over the past days.

"So I found," he muttered. Khalvir lapsed into silence, awaiting an explanation for her absence. He felt she owed him one, though he could not guess why. Her business was not his concern.

She shifted where she crouched. "I'm sorry I did not come yesterday," she offered in apology, but no further explanation of her absence was forthcoming.

Huh. He tried not to feel concerned for the worry that did not leave her eyes. Something had happened. He could feel it.

"Here." She offered him a tiny piece of root. It did not even fill her open palm.

Khalvir frowned as his stomach rumbled. Two days of not eating and this was all she could bring? He chose not to say anything. "Thank you, she-elf."

"Nyriaana," she tried. "It's Nyri. Can't you remember, Juaan?"

He knew what she was called, but he shuddered away from the sound of it. "Khalvir," he reminded her sternly. "And of course I don't."

He had to get her off this subject. He bit into her offering. The bitter tang, same flavour as those foul roots he had expelled from the pit, seeped onto his tongue. Khalvir resisted the urge to spit. He forced the bite down his throat without really chewing. "This is awful! What is this?"

His discomfort was almost worth the bitterness when his reaction drew a smile from her, the expression of dread on her face dispelling for a brief moment. "Gora root." She explained as her lips twisted in amusement. "It's very good for you. Makes you big and strong."

"Whoever told you that complete and total—?"

"Never mind." She cut him off with a shake of her head. "It's a private joke. Just eat."

He had faced worse hardships. He ate the vile root.

By and by Khalvir realised she was staring at him again in that way she had of making him feel very self-conscious. "What?"

She reached a hand towards his face. Part of him wanted to let her touch him, to feel her warm skin on his again. The other half of him knew that was why he had to resist. He shied away. Her lips pulled down as she dropped her rejected hand. Instead, she touched her fingers to her own chin. "You have hair here."

"Yes," he said, raising an eyebrow at her query.

She shook her head in wonder. "It's... strange. I've seen nothing like it before."

Surprise flickered through him. "Your people don't grow beards?" Khalvir sifted through his memories of every elf male he had ever seen. He realised none had ever had a beard.

"Beards?" she tested the word on her lips.

The look of puzzlement on her face was so endearing, so innocent, Khalvir found he could not be annoyed by her continued scrutiny. "You are very strange, elf," he said, amused.

Her embarrassment was evident, and Khalvir saw the defensiveness deepen the frown sitting between her brows. "What is this *elf*?"

"That's what you are, aren't you?" he provoked her with her own previous words to him. "It's what we call you."

Her reaction was better than Khalvir expected. Her chin lifted fiercely. "I am not an *elf*. My People are the Ninkuraaja, created by the holy Ninmah."

She had to know how pompous that sounded.

"Oh, really." Khalvir raised his eyebrows. He was enjoying this more than he cared to admit. His heart thrilled at the sight of the vital reactions in her eyes when he had thought to never see them again. He drank everything in.

"So what do *Woves* call themselves?" she huffed.

Her words punctured his enjoyment and his face fell, realising he had been letting himself go too far. "We have clan names." Khalvir looked down at the remaining *gora* root in his hand, searching for a way to change the subject. "Is this all you can bring to eat?"

This reaction he did not expect. Fury blazed in her eyes. Before Khalvir could blink, she was on her feet, leaning over him, shaking with anger. "Yes, as a matter of fact, it is!" she spat. "Thanks to your *clan*, we now no longer have enough food to get us through the Fury. You took most everything. You are lucky to get that, believe me, *Forbidden*."

It was the first time she had looked at him in such a way, like he truly was her enemy. Khalvir was amazed at how much that wounded him. He mulled over her words. Only now did he realise her face was very different from the first time he had seen her. She was half the weight she had been; her cheekbones stood out too clearly.

Who knew what she had to go through to bring him this food, the bare remains of what his raiding party had left them with. The hardship of the elves would once have meant little. They were heartless enemies that Khalvir cared nothing for. Now the suffering he had caused was plain to see. She was starving on her feet.

"I'm sorry," he said, meaning for so much more than his careless words. "That was wrong of me."

"Huh," she grunted. "Small comfort that is to the old and the young who will die this Fury from starvation." She stopped as her voice cracked upon the last.

It tore at his heart. "I'm sorry."

Khalvir knew his words would never be enough, but her anger burned out. She sank back to the ground, spent, looking far older than her scant seasons. "No, I'm sorry," she sighed, staring at the ground. "You don't need to hear."

Khalvir shifted uncomfortably. He had nothing to offer her to make up for his crimes, except— "Are you hungry?"

She shook her head. "No."

He almost laughed at the role reversal. Well, two could play at this game.

"Here." Khalvir moved to break off a piece of the root for her. He had forgotten about his broken fingers. Pain sliced up his arm as he tried to use his hand. He could not control his reaction as his features twisted.

She did not miss it. "Let me heal that." She offered her hand.

Instinctive fear seized him, and he drew away. She was seeking to use her power on him. His all but forgotten resentment rose once more.

"Please," she appealed. "I don't like to see you in pain."

Khalvir looked at her hand, then his own and back again, torn.

"Please. Please trust me." She stretched her hand out further. So fragile, so vulnerable. His hand was reaching for her fingers before he could think to stop himself. Confusion swamped him at this uncontrollable need to protect her. Her eyes pleaded with him, begging him to understand something beyond his reach.

Khalvir's resistance crumbled. "I'll let you heal me, but only if you eat something. You look like the wind could blow you away." And he placed his hand in hers, feeling an instant relief as he did so, as if an incomplete part of his soul was now whole and healed by her very presence.

Joy brightened her entire face.

He held very still as she worked. He could feel the whisperings of energy against his latent senses. Senses he usually ignored and pushed deep down. Khalvir had always refused to acknowledge any part of him that was elven. He held his breath, expecting pain or at least discomfort, but there was nothing. Only an easing of the agony, like cool water washing over his hand. The bones in his fingers tingled pleasantly as she finished.

Khalvir took his hand back and stared at what she had done. When she had healed his leg, he had not been conscious. Now that he had witnessed her power at work, how easily she had mended shattered bones, anger and resentment flooded through him. It brought home to him how that elf had—

He couldn't even let himself think of it. He felt hot tears prick in the corners of his eyes. That day had convinced him above all others that the elves were a despicable race and his Chief's beliefs were no more than madness.

Despite the rage coursing through him, none of it could be directed at her. This elf at least had a heart. "Never believed it," the murmur came unbidden.

She caught his unguarded moment. "Never believed what?"

Khalvir forced his grief and bitterness back into the darkest recesses of his heart and smoothed his expression. "You elves have a great power."

"I am not an *elf*. I am of the Ninkuraaja."

"Yes." He smiled. "That's a bit of a mouthful."

She grinned. "It took you a long time to teach me how to say it properly." She shook her head at his reproachful frown. "Never mind."

"Thank you."

"You're welcome." She smiled at his heart-felt thanks.

Khalvir dropped his eyes as his bruised heart squeezed at the sight of her smile. It only increased her beauty. He continued studying his hand instead. She was a powerful and skilled healer. Here he was, sitting with everything his Chief hoped to possess.

The thought of this girl in his Chief's grasp flitted through his mind and it filled Khalvir with a sudden despair that sucked his breath away. He could never allow it. He thought of the returning whistle he had detected on the barest edges of his awareness two nights before and regretted for the first time that his men were searching for him.

"Thank me for that by not trying to escape again." Her voice broke into his brooding.

He raised his eyebrows at her. He should try to escape. He should get as far away from here as possible. If they found her with him—

"I mean it." Her lips twitched. "Please, promise me you'll stay here and keep quiet. I wasn't lying when I said the Elders had posted extra watch. They may patrol around close by. You cannot do anything to attract their attention. Please, for me, stay quiet and wait for my return. I will not leave you to die. Trust me."

And he did. He did not know when it had happened, but that secret part of himself that he did not want to acknowledge had finally won out. Khalvir would trust this girl with his life. The thought of leaving her now, despite the danger of being with him put her in, was unbearable.

"What is it about you, elf?" he murmured. He wasn't in control of himself anymore. He could no longer fight and, though his higher self screamed at the wrongness of it, he gave her his word. "I promise."

"Thank you." She looked relieved. "They will kill you if they find you and I could not bear it if they did." Her small hand came towards him again. The expression in her eyes made Khalvir's heart pound, and he leaned away from her once more, frightened by what he felt. This time, she ignored his resistance and placed her fingertips against his cheek.

Khalvir was not prepared for what happened next. His skin blazed under her touch, the intensity of his feelings exploding, doubling in strength; her emotions were now his. He could feel her there, inside his heart. He could feel *everything*. Never had Khalvir experienced anything like this, and it left him breathless. She loved him with an intensity that hurt. Her words floated down to him as though from a great distance. "I can't lose you again. Ever. You mean too much to me."

Khalvir pulled back, breaking the connection. He was aware of the wide-eyed surprise that was frozen upon his face, but he was quite unable to do anything about it. He could not speak.

Embarrassment coloured her expression at his lack of response. She dropped her eyes and left without a backwards glance, leaving him staring at the space she had occupied, bewildered and confused.

That night when a querying whistle came floating through the blackness, Khalvir did not raise his head to respond.

***

CHAPTER 11

DECEPTION

"Khalvir is out there waiting for us," Galahir insisted as he faced the rest of the men.

"You can't know that, Galahir."

"I *know* I heard him," Galahir argued. "Banahir called, and he answered."

All eyes now turned to Banahir. The other man shrugged. "We heard what we thought was a whistle three nights past, but it was very faint. We might have been mistaken."

"It *was* him." Galahir insisted. He refused to let the doubt that had crept into the minds of the rest of the men sink into his own.

"Why have we not heard anything since, then?"

"I don't know." Galahir blew out a breath.

Even he had to admit, since that first tenuous contact, they had heard no further response from their missing leader. It was getting harder to convince the others that these invasions into the forest were worth risking the wrath of the witches for. Every time they searched in the western parts of the forest, the wolves were waiting to block their path. Most of the men had become so spooked by the eerie line of silent sentinels that half of them now refused to obey Galahir's wishes to re-enter the forest.

"Perhaps he cannot respond. Perhaps the elves are close and he cannot draw attention to himself. There could be countless reasons for him to remain silent." Galahir could see the skepticism on their faces, even as he spoke.

"They watch us every time we breach their borders. They are plotting something, Galahir. We have been pushing our luck. We need to stop now and wait until Lorhir returns with the Chief's orders."

"It could be too late by then!"

"Then what do you propose we do?" Ranab threw his hands up.

"I don't know!" Galahir punched at a tree in frustration. He was not the decision maker. He struggled to think of what Khalvir would do if he was here, but his thoughts hazed uselessly.

His stomach growled. He had eaten before entering the forest on his latest search, but hunger was gnawing at his insides once again. One thing he knew for sure was, if Khalvir was here, he would have made some joke about Galahir's constant need for food.

He looked to the campfire, but saw to his disappointment that there was no meat roasting over the licking tongues.

"We ran out of rations." Ranab read the longing upon his face. "All we have left is this." Banahir's younger brother gestured to the baskets full of fruits, nuts and roots that they had seized from the elven settlement.

Galahir wrinkled his nose. He had no stomach for such fare. He needed the nourishment of hot, juicy flesh between his teeth to satisfy his burly frame. This food of the elves was to be a tribute to the rest of the clan and the Chief. It would not do to deplete it before their return.

Galahir sighed. Weary as he was, there was nothing for it but to hunt. Food would help clear his thoughts.

"Gather some spears," he gestured to Banahir and Ranab. "We'll hunt further out on the plains. We will find no game in the forest without forfeiting our lives."

Galahir took point as they set out across the frosty ground, the browned grasses crunching satisfyingly under his feet. The cool, fresh air swept through his lungs, exhilarating him. *This* was where he was supposed to be, unfettered by trees and undergrowth. Free. Free to run and breathe.

A herd of deer was the first thing they came across. Galahir gestured for the men to keep low as they assessed the herd's numbers and looked for weaknesses.

"There," Ranab pointed. "A young buck. He's been lamed."

Galahir and Banahir followed the other man's direction and spied the beast he had singled out. It was near the back of the herd, struggling to keep its position as it limped along on one front leg.

Perfect.

It would take careful timing to separate it from the rest of the herd. Galahir gestured, indicating Ranab should circle around to the other side of the deer, then motioned a pincer movement between Banahir and Ranab. The other two pure Cro men were far swifter than him.

They would come at the herd from both sides and cut off the straggler. Galahir would then come from behind and strike. Hunting big game was a skill Galahir excelled at. Without question, the other two men did as he directed.

Keeping downwind, Ranab moved around the herd and dropped into position. Timing was everything. Break too soon and all would be lost. Galahir held his breath as Banahir and Ranab stalked forward, slinking as close to the herd as possible before breaking their cover.

They were each fifteen paces away from the herd when the lead doe lifted her head and sniffed the air. Singing out, she cried an alarm, but it was too late. Galahir sounded his own message, and the other two men sprang as the herd bolted. The injured animal at the back had nowhere to go as the three men cut off its escape.

Galahir aimed and ended it quickly, hurling his spear directly at the beast's heart. His aim struck true and the young buck toppled to the ground as Galahir rushed forward and cut its throat with his hunting knife. The buck was dead within moments.

A holler of celebration went up from Banahir and Ranab. Galahir grinned. The buck was large. It would feed the remains of their raiding group for days if they cleaned it in time. This was not the place for such a job, however.

"Let's get it back to camp. Spear-tooths could be on the prowl."

Banahir and Ranab moved towards the carcass, but Galahir waved them away, trying not to look too satisfied as he lifted the heavy carcass from the ground and slung it effortlessly across his shoulders. They could look down on his Thal heritage all they wanted, but they could not sneer at the sheer brute strength it gave him.

The men that had remained at camp cheered softly as Galahir's hunting group returned with their spoils and Galahir thumped their prize upon the ground in triumph. The men were quick to set to work, skinning and cleaning the catch. It wasn't long before the first round of cooking meat was sizzling over the fire.

Bellies full at last, Galahir watched as they all lay back in contentment. There was one question, however, that still needed to be answered, and he could see the expectation clearly on their faces.

"What is your decision, Galahir?" Banahir asked and Galahir knew they were all hoping he would decide not to go back into the forest and continue with the futile task of finding Khalvir alive. He gritted his teeth. They would not be happy when he disappointed them.

"That settlement lies to the west, I know it. The elves watch us wherever we go, and do nothing, but when we turn west, that is when the wolves appear. They are protecting something. We need to get past them."

"And how, in Ea's name, do you propose we do that?"

Galahir had been thinking long and hard about the issue. The hunt out on the open plains and a satisfying meal had had the desired effect of clearing his head. He thought he had the beginnings of an idea.

The previous nights' excursions had at least achieved the result of eliminating a lot of territory from their search. Galahir was getting to know the forest now. But he could not search as he wanted with the elves peering over his shoulder and blocking his movements. He needed to think of a way to throw their scent off somehow.

"We need to get in without the elves notice. They have got used to us sending in only one search at a time." Galahir voiced his idea slowly. "If we sent in one search party to draw their sentries away, they may not be expecting a second to follow."

"That's a big leap, Galahir."

Galahir knew it wasn't the best plan, but it was the only one he had. "It's worth a try. We'll put it to the test tonight."

There were murmurs of discontent. Galahir looked around the group, but all avoided his gaze.

"We're not going back in there without reinforcements, Galahir." Ranab spoke for them all. "The next time we go in," the younger man shook his head, "we won't be walking back out. You have been foolish, putting our lives at risk as you have."

Galahir raised his chin as his cheeks flushed. "Then I will go back alone."

A sigh sounded from the edge of the campfire. "Trying to shame us all with your boar-headed courage as usual, Galahir?" Banahir said. Galahir opened his mouth, but the other man cut him off before he could formulate a response. "Very well. I'll help you this one last time, Galahir. One. Last. Just tell me what you want to do."

***

CHAPTER 12

SHADOWS

The prevailing days were awkward. Neither could look the other in the eye, following the outpouring of emotion that had taken place after the witch had healed his fingers. When she was not with him, Khalvir paced the pit restlessly. He was falling. He was falling for her.

All his resistance had come to nothing. He had been lying to himself in thinking he ever had a chance. She had possessed him utterly from the first moment he had laid eyes on her. Never had he allowed such feelings. Never since— He banished the terrible memory.

Khalvir knew there were women in his clan who wanted him. He was not oblivious to their admiring stares; the desire reserved for only the strongest of men. The likes of Kikima made such a thing impossible. There were those who wanted him to Challenge for them, who wanted to be Claimed as his mate. But he resisted, paying their advances little mind, no matter how persistent; his lips twisted. He could not do it. The scars of what his Chief had once made him do still haunted him too badly. He remembered too well how that had ended.

Khalvir came up against a wall and pounded his fist against the rock in frustration. Every hardship that had befallen him had been because of his elven blood. How he wished he could be rid of it. And here he was, falling for an elven girl as she tore down all of his defences.

He resumed pacing. His fear of her falling into the possession of his Chief was increasing by the day. He knew what he should do. He should drive her away, he should make her leave him. But his heart screamed at the thought, imagining the pain he would have to cause her. But if it saved her...

Khalvir closed his eyes. He could not face the choice now. Leaves rustled above. She had returned.

They chewed on the food she had brought in, the silence that had become almost customary. Khalvir was not sure how to break it. He could not think of what to say to her.

There was more colour in her cheeks today, and she looked stronger than she had in a long time. He had been fearing that she would fade away right in front of him. In the last days, she had looked barely capable of standing; the rations she brought barely enough to keep a child alive. He had said nothing, though. He had not wanted to upset her again.

Today it pleased him to see she had brought more, handing over two whole fruits. Her features, however, were no less drawn. There was an aura of guilt hanging over her as she gifted the food. He felt a shiver of concern. What had these extra rations cost her?

"I have to leave now," she finally broke the silence and Khalvir realised their time was already up. "I'm not sure when I can return. Things are about to get a little complicated."

He wondered how much more complicated things could get. "Why?" Disappointment thudded through him. Her visits were the only thing that got him through each long, mindlessly boring day.

Her face twisted. "My... kinswoman," she explained, "lost her baby on the night your clan came..."

Khalvir's mind flashed back to that fateful night, to the very first time he had seen her. He would never forget her brandishing a stick at him as she stood in front of the pregnant girl crumpled upon the forest floor. "The girl who fell from the tree?" he clarified.

"Yes." Her reply was bitter, clipped.

So... the other girl had survived her terrible fall but lost the baby. Khalvir could not help but feel responsible for yet another pain he had caused her. The elf drew a steadying breath. "I have been bound by my teacher to take over her care because she cannot yet be left alone, she is grieving too deeply."

"Your teacher?"

"Yes. In the art of healing. Baarias—"

The flashes of colour and emotion went off inside him. Over the days, Khalvir had grown numb to her use of the name Juaan, so much so that his heart barely reacted anymore. This new name was fresh. Raw. It felt familiar in more ways than one; it shivered darkly through him. "Baarias? That is his name?"

A strange emotion crossed her face at his reaction. She looked hurt, though he could not fathom why. "Yes," she answered. "What of it?"

He tried to push away the feelings of anger and resentment the name evoked. There was something else, too. It nagged at his mind. He had heard that name before. "He must be a skilful master," he muttered.

"Yes, he is." There was a reverent note of respect in her voice. He could feel her eyes on him, but did not look up. "I promise I will come back. Wait for me."

Baarias. The name shivered through him again, a shadow on his soul, indistinct, insubstantial, impossible to grasp. For once, Khalvir barely noticed when she left.

CHAPTER 13

BELIEFS

K halvir slept restlessly. The rock at his back was relentless, as was the constant noise from the forest. He could not close it out, no matter how hard he tried. Once again, he longed for the stark solitude of the plains. He wondered how much longer it was until dawn. Too long. The silver circle of Nanna was high overhead. He could just make out the cold light, flickering and filtering down through the canopy to steal through the gaps in the pit's cover above.

Would she come? She had said things were about to become *complicated* and did not know when she could return. The prospect of having nothing to break up the tedium, of not seeing her for any length of time soured his outlook considerably.

Khalvir sank deeper into his furs and tried to find rest. He hadn't realised he had actually fallen asleep until the sound of her voice roused him. "Juaan. Juaan?"

He really wished she would stop calling him that. He could see her slight form turning uncertainly a few strides from him. It didn't appear that she could see him in the dark. "Khalvir," he corrected, rising to his feet.

She froze, her whole body locking down. He saw her fists clench and heard her breathing quicken. Was she afraid? He put a hand out and touched her shoulder. She flinched violently. It stung him she would be so fearful of him.

"It's all right," he soothed. "Don't be alarmed, elf. I promised I would not hurt you." Khalvir lifted his hand away from her shoulder and held both up in the air, displaying he meant no harm.

She breathed again. "Nyri," she reminded him.

"Khalvir, then." He moved away from her to sit back against the rock wall. She followed him, blindly it seemed, for she trod on him. "That was my foot."

"Well," she danced backwards. A stone clattered in the dark. "Ow! Don't clothe yourself in damned black, then."

He laughed softly at her annoyance. "I have little choice, really. It's either that or go naked down here."

Khalvir could almost feel the heat rise on her skin and gated another laugh at her embarrassment. Her next words distracted him, however. "If you were Ninkuraaja, I'd know exactly where every part of you was without having to see you."

"Truly? You cannot sense me, then?"

"Well, I can, but not exactly." She sat down within an arm's length of him. Khalvir's skin prickled at her nearness. The urge to reach out and touch her was so powerful he struggled to stay focused on her words. "It's like a part of you... an energy... for want of a better word, is not there or lies dormant, if you see what I mean."

"Not really," he lied. She could not know of the beast that lurked inside him.

She sighed. "It is hard to explain. How do you describe seeing to a blind man?"

"How indeed." Khalvir turned his head to study her, wishing he could see her beautiful face more clearly, the spark in her indigo eyes. She seemed to sense his gaze on her and her hand came out, holding forth his ration for the day. It was the middle of the night, but he was still hungry. He took the offering and bit into it. A familiar, bitter tang filling his mouth.

"Not this again," he complained.

"Eat and be grateful."

He grumbled, but said nothing. There was still an underlying pain in her voice whenever the subject of food arose. He didn't want to make things harder for her than they already were; he knew there was much she wasn't telling him.

A chirruping whistle cut through the air. Khalvir froze. His men were closer tonight. Closer than ever before.

Her head came up. "What is that? I have never heard such a bird before."

Khalvir shrugged and kept his face impassive. He could not let her leave him while his men were in the forest. They were so close tonight that she could run into them on her way back to her People. He closed his eyes.

"So, what have you been up to today?"

Khalvir nearly choked on his root. *Really?* He guessed a need to break the lengthening silence drove her question rather than any real interest in what he might have been up to, trapped at the bottom of a featureless hole. "Not climbing if that's what you're worried about."

She snorted. "I'm always worried. You're just the latest on top of a great pile of concerns."

Khalvir was about to respond when a howl ripped through the air somewhere in the near distance. The sound of it made the hair on his neck stand on end. The dreaded sound was long and piercing. It was not his men this time. He knew what that sound meant. Khalvir leaped to his feet.

"It's only the wolves," a soft voice whispered, unnaturally devoid of fear. "They are hunting."

"That's what scares me," Khalvir replied tersely. At least he was grateful for one thing. If the wolves were on the prowl, his men would not stay in the area.

But he was trapped here, defenceless and alone. A cold sweat started on his brow as he felt the predators' nearness.

"They do not hunt us," the witch reassured. "The wolves, like every Child of the Great Spirit of KI, are our cousins and teachers. They do no harm."

Khalvir's feeling of vulnerability made him suddenly irritable with her cool lack of concern. "Not to you, perhaps, with your witch magic," he retorted. "But I have known those beasts to take the old and the very young and devour them if the strong are not watchful. They are one of our most bitter enemies and we will kill them in turn."

He thought he felt her shudder. He knew he'd struck another of her elf sensibilities when her voice grew hard. "The Woves are the unnatural creation of Ninsiku." She bit back. "I'm not surprised KI sends his Children to kill them. All of Ninsiku's creations are bloodthirsty abominations. They are not the People of Ninmah. They do not have the Gift. They do not hear."

His anger flared. "So all the bloody losses we have suffered are our own fault, are they? Just for being who we are? Typical elf. Such creatures are monsters who cannot be reasoned with, only their savage hunger drives them. They cannot speak. They do not think!"

"Of course they do!" she argued hotly. Khalvir could not mistake her passion burning just beneath the surface. "They speak with the voice and truth of the earth. How can you look at everything around you and say there is no thought behind it? The world is alive with the greatest of intelligence. We are blind to it unless we learn to use Ninmah's Gift to us. The Woves are the ones who do not know how to speak. They are the monsters. Abominations on the earth and they have blinded you, too. You *used* to understand."

Khalvir had stopped listening, afraid of losing his temper any further. He would never make her understand. Not like this. Her prejudices against his People were too strong. *Monsters.* His lips twisted bitterly. If only she knew. He had to change the subject.

"Who is this KI?" he asked instead. He couldn't quite keep the sullen tone from his voice. "And Ninmah and Ninsiku? More elven superstition?"

Her shock at his words was so strong even he could feel it. "You do not know who Ninsiku is?" Her voice was sharp. "He is the very power that created the Woves."

More of her misconceptions. "Well, if he did he's kept silent about it."

She leaped to her feet and paced the pit. His words had agitated her somehow.

"What's wrong?"

"You *must* know Ninsiku," she hissed. "It is the Woves who give him his power. It is they who are providing him with the strength to overthrow Ninmah, to wipe us out, and bring about the End of Days where eternal cold and darkness hold sway."

Khalvir sat, absorbing her words. So this was what the elves believed? This was what they saw? He turned the concept over in his mind. He supposed the ruthlessness of his Chief had done nothing to remedy this opinion. Maybe here, now, he could make this girl see. They were not the monsters her People saw. "I have never heard of

Ninsiku," he informed her. "We do not do his bidding, nor do we worship him."

Her hands were shaking as she ran them through her dark hair. "Then why are we suffering?" she demanded. "It has only happened since the Woves arrived. If Ninsiku does not command them, why do they hunt us? Why do they come and take our young, as the wolves come for theirs, to devour in the night?"

Khalvir could not prevent the laugh that barked from his throat. "*Devour* you? What a ridiculous notion. Is that what you believe?"

"What else are we supposed to believe?" she shot back. "The Woves come. They sacrifice our homes to their burning spirits. They kill and kidnap. Flesh eaters! If they do not devour us, if Ninsiku does not send them, why do they come?"

He studied his recently healed fingers. He could not believe they had not figured it out. "You truly do not know?" he asked softly.

"What is there to know? All we know is that they come and kill us."

Khalvir sighed and dropped his hand. She was very upset. He was obviously digging into her greatest pain. It was not her fault she believed what she did. "Please, sit," he invited. "Talk to me. Who is KI? We know little of your superstitions." He had to keep her talking, keep her with him until he was sure the others had left this part of the forest. He strained his ears, listening for any further signs.

She was drawing deep breaths, attempting to regain her composure. "That's a very long story," she growled, irritated.

Khalvir snorted. Perfect. "It's not like I've got anywhere to go, thanks to you. What do you think I have to do between your brief visits? At least give me something to think about."

She sighed rather impatiently. His words had truly upset her. She was debating whether she wanted to continue talking to him. Khalvir saw her glance up out of the pit and he grew afraid that she was about to leave. He couldn't let her go.

"Is KI your guiding light?" he prompted. He wanted her to know he was not mocking her. He was genuinely interested now.

"The KI is everything." His tone seemed to have swayed her. To his relief, she settled back down by his side and Khalvir felt again that odd sense of completeness; it felt so right to be near her. Her voice was hushed with reverence as she spoke. "He is the Great Spirit of the earth. He exists in the rocks and the ground beneath our feet, flowing in great Rivers that criss-cross the land, guiding his Children on their journeys. He lives in the trees that surround us. He moves as the wolf and the deer. He is Life itself."

"Ah," Khalvir said thoughtfully. "And how do you know this? Do you see him?"

"*Feel* him is probably a better way to speak of it. Though... when I am still, with my eyes closed, he usually appears as a golden energy flowing through everything that exists. He can be felt the strongest when close to the Rivers. This forest lies along one such Line. Everything is a part of the great power that flows through the earth."

"Interesting," he murmured. "Does that include you and I?"

The elf-witch shook her head. "We are different. We are not the Great Spirit's children. The Ninkuraaja are the People of Ninmah, the great Queen and Healer and She made the essence of the Great Spirit a part of us. She alone knew how to give her People Sight. Only by using Ninmah's Gift are we able to glimpse the Great Spirit, to learn and look after his secrets. Ninmah made us for that purpose."

Khalvir raised his brows sceptically. He thought of the gods of old who had supposedly come from the sky to create man in all his forms, only to abandon him. His People had long since turned their backs on them and their teachings. No one had ever seen one of these *gods* or witnessed their power. He did not believe they had ever even existed. He did not mention this to her though, it would only upset her again. "Ninmah's gift?" he prompted.

She sighed and gathered herself. Khalvir could tell he was in for a long story. Her voice rolled out, weaving the story of Ninmah and the first of her People. She told of how they had been Gifted with a special power to hear the voice of the Great Spirit of the earth. She spoke so passionately, he could almost believe it, almost see it all. At times she sang, and the sound was so beautiful it hurt his heart. She truly was a magical being.

"Ninmah's Gift is our higher thought," she concluded, "a connection between mind and soul. Ninmah showed us how to reach out to the Children of the Great Spirit and His world by connecting with the essence of Him she used to create the Ninkuraaja soul." She placed a hand over her heart. "We are blessed to be able to hear the Great Spirit's song."

Khalvir stared at her, watching her face in the dimness. Again he was filled with the need to reach out and touch her, to quench this yearning deep in his soul. "You tell a good story," he whispered. "It's... nice... listening to your voice." The admission was out of his mouth before he could stop it.

Their eyes locked. A flush crept up her cheeks and her fingers twitched as though she very much wanted to touch him, too. Khalvir's heart beat faster as his desire burned. He was about to lean forward, to press his mouth to hers, when she looked up, cocking her head. The spell was broken and Khalvir leaned back hastily. What was he *thinking*?

"Listen," she said, as more and more howls joined the voices of the night. "It's beautiful, isn't it? Can't you hear Him?"

"No," Khalvir said. His voice sounded strained to his own ears. He rubbed his forehead. He felt dizzy. "You said we *Woves* are Ninsiku's creation? And you believe us to be evil."

"Yes, they are." Her reply came quick and certain. "Ninmah's brethren created their own Peoples, but they were born Blind. They could not know the Great Spirit and so they were made powerful in other ways. Ninsiku was Ninmah's mate, and he grew full of jealousy and spite. He created the Woves with dark energies to oppose Ninmah's People. They are nothing but evil spirits clothed in flesh."

Khalvir smiled. "I suppose I can see why you would believe that." He looked her right in the eye. Surely, after this time with him, she could see that such beliefs were flawed. Surely she saw he wasn't a monster. "And what do you think now?" He challenged quietly. "Do you still see me as an evil spirit clothed in flesh? I am one of your *Woves*. What do you think now?"

"You are no Wove, Juaan," she said stubbornly. "They took you and made you their servant. Your mother was a Ninkuraa. Your father was..." she trailed off, frowning heavily.

Khalvir turned away, stung. She was still wrapped up in the belief that he was someone else entirely. She did not see *him*. It was not him she loved. When she eventually saw her mistake, she would leave him. The thought was not pleasant. "What became of Ninsiku and Ninmah?" he asked, finally.

"Ninsiku came to destroy us and Ninmah fought him. The power of their battle would have destroyed the earth. Ninmah saw that the only way to make us safe was to leave with Her erstwhile mate. She imprisoned him in the heavens and exiled Herself along with him to hold his dark power in balance. For time out of memory, they have continued to chase one another through the sky. Ninmah's spirit appears as the Golden Mother by day until She has to give way to

Ninsiku. The night is his." She pointed warily to the silver crescent in the sky. "His eye watches us in the darkness, surrounded by the lights of the souls he has stolen. We are best to avoid him lest he see us and send his dark servants."

Khalvir rose and stepped into the cold light pouring through the gap in the pit's coverings that she had made. He held his hands out, studying the light spilling across them. Nothing but harmless light. "This is your Ninsiku?"

She had huddled into the corner, seemingly wanting to disappear into the rock's embrace. "Yes," she whispered. "He sees all. Ready to steal away the unwary."

Khalvir frowned. Elves feared the night's spirit. He had never feared the night but her terror was obvious; he was scaring her by standing where he was. He shrugged and moved back into the shadows with her. "Best not to be caught in his stare then." He sat. "I never realised what interesting beliefs you elves had."

"What beliefs do the Woves have?" she whispered. "What powers do they possess?"

Khalvir considered his words for a long time, wondering if what he had to say would upset her again. He was about to contradict everything she believed. "Our beliefs are not entirely dissimilar. We believe our People were created by gods that came from the sky. Ea created our People to serve him as Ninhursag, his twin sister of the Sky, created yours. But unlike you, we don't believe our creators left for our best interests.

"In our legends, they left to live in the mountains where no man can tread and forsook all contact, aside from descending occasionally to kidnap women. We had grown tiresome to them. Yet still we continued to cling loyally to the wisdom they had taught us for many generations.

"But then the Great Winter of Sorrow came and nearly wiped us all out. Ea did not return. Lost and without hope, we turned our backs on the teachings of the traitorous gods. It served us well, and we have grown strong enough to survive without them. But now, once again, the world is shifting." Khalvir gave a bitter laugh. "I'm sorry to shatter your cosy illusion of blame, but we have no power to lend a supposed god who brings the cold, elf. We pray for Ninmah, as you call her, to regain strength and push back the winter. But she does not listen any more than Ea."

Khalvir tilted his head back against the rock wall. "Perhaps we are being punished for having the audacity to survive when they clearly did not wish it but, either way, I fear the world we know is dying and there is nothing that you or I or anyone else can do to stop it."

The witch did not answer. He watched her as the darkness faded to grey, but her expression remained troubled, her thoughts hidden from him.

It was nearing dawn when she finally left him.

"When will you be back?" The need to reach out and pull her back to him, to keep her safe within the protection of his arms, was almost too much to resist. Khalvir could not bear the thought of her out in the unknown without him. But he had heard no more calls from his men, and he could think of nothing else to delay her.

"When Ninsiku rises again, I will return. Wait for me."

A smile spread over his face. "For as long as these walls stand... Nyriaana." Her name burned upon his lips. "Keep the wolves close."

She appeared somewhat dazed as she clambered up her root.

Stay safe, come back to me. Khalvir watched her until she was gone.

***

Chapter 14

ATTACK

It had worked better than Galahir had hoped. Banahir had entered the forest at dawn ahead of him. The other man had not been happy at the prospect of going alone, but none of the other men could be persuaded.

After Banahir had disappeared, Galahir had waited for his turn, counting his heartbeats. He had to be sure the elves did not expect a second intrusion and focused all of their attention on Banahir, leaving Galahir free to search wherever he wanted.

They had taken the bait. Banahir had led them to the east. Galahir had headed west, revelling in the freedom of not having the sense of malevolent eyes crawling up his back.

Utu rose in the sky above him as he searched, whistling out every so often, hoping to receive an answer. Khalvir did not respond, but the light of day gave Galahir the clarity he needed to see his surroundings.

The wolves were not there to block his path this time and as he travelled further west than he had yet been able to venture. He listened carefully. Sure enough, he could hear the telltale sound of the river babbling; a background noise to the constant din of the forest. The same as they had heard on that fateful night when they had found the witches' settlement. Galahir's heart beat double time as he ran towards the sound.

The river was wide but shallow. Coming upon its banks, Galahir quickly stooped, removed the oxen skull from his head and drank his fill, splashing water on his hot, sticky face as he did so. There was hardly any breeze through the trees to shift the heavy atmosphere.

Refreshed, Galahir studied the area. If he followed this river upstream, then he would eventually find what he had been looking for. Shoving the skull back into place over his sandy hair, Galahir gathered his *arshu* and struck out in his chosen direction.

Utu was somewhere high overhead when he picked up the first signs that his instincts had proven correct. Then he heard the voices. Elven voices.

Dropping low, Galahir crept forward on hands and feet and peered over the undergrowth. His heart leaped as he beheld at last the massive trees that the elves called home.

It took all of his restraint not to go charging forward, *arshu* in hand, and mount a rescue attack. He didn't need Khalvir to tell him what a foolhardy move that would be. Galahir was amazed he had got as close as he had without being detected. He had expected the settlement to be heavily guarded since their raid. All the sentries must have been sent to tail Banahir. This had worked out better than he had hoped.

Galahir sank down into the undergrowth, careful to keep out of sight as he settled in to observe.

He was shocked to see how few of the elves there were. As Utu passed overhead, he only counted ten elves. Most were dark headed with the occasional silver-hair to be seen climbing up or down one of the numerous trees. Galahir watched their behaviour closely, searching for any hint that Khalvir was being held captive in any of their strange dwellings. None were being guarded that he could see.

Galahir debated with himself and then risked giving out a soft, querying whistle. If Khalvir was present, he would hear Galahir's signal and respond.

He sank further into the undergrowth when several pairs of curious eyes lifted at the sound of the strange birdlike call. It had been a risk. The elves would know every bird in their forest and could tell instantly if a sound was out of place. The gamble did not pay off, for there came no reply. He dared not risk another call.

Letting out a frustrated breath, Galahir observed the elven settlement for a while longer before concluding that Khalvir was not there. It would be unwise to remain any longer. Banahir would most likely have left the forest by now and the elven sentries could return at any moment.

Backing up carefully, Galahir disappeared back into the outer forest. Disappointment thudded through him. He had been so certain that if he located the settlement, then he would find Khalvir. The doubt that the answering whistle he had heard several nights previously had been real sank into his heart.

He headed further east as Utu waned overhead. He could not resist letting out a few more calls as he went.

Silence.

Galahir kicked at the earth. Even though he knew his time was up, he still could not bring himself to leave the forest and return to camp. He did not want to see the vindication on the other men's faces when he once again returned empty-handed. This had been his last chance. He shouldered through some tall underbrush, wondering where he should search next.

"Ah!" Galahir gave a soft yelp as something stung his arm. Glancing back, he saw the creature responsible. The yellow frog gleamed upon the leaves he had just disturbed, spines bristling from its gleaming skin. Galahir's own skin flared as though burned, punctured by the aggressive hopper. "Ah," he hissed again, wrapping his other hand around the injury. But it was too late. Exhaustion swept over him. *Oh no.*

Poisoned.

Galahir staggered as the effects of the frog's toxin swept through his body. *Adamu above!* Sinking down against a tree before he fell, Galahir laid his head back against the trunk as the darkness closed over him.

The sound of a whistle startled him awake. Gasping in shock, Galahir leaped to his feet, gritting his teeth as his vision swam. He was relieved to discover that he was alive, but he felt like he had drained several skins of vision water. His heart sank when he realised how long the hopper's poison had robbed him of his senses. The surrounding forest was now dark. Wolves were howling in the distance and the hairs on his arms rose in response.

It was not the wolves that had woken him, though. It had been a hunting whistle. Someone was calling him.

Khalvir?

Before he could form another thought, the signal sounded again. It was close. Galahir grabbed his *arshu* from where it had fallen at his feet and staggered off in the call's direction.

He slowed when he felt the familiar unpleasant prickle run up his spine. An elf was nearby. Galahir cast around, hardly daring to breathe. *Where are you?*

Then he saw him. It was a dark-haired male, perched in the low branches of a tree. His skin and clothes camouflaged him so well that Galahir needed to scan the same place twice before he picked him out.

Galahir ducked out of sight. The elf hadn't seen him. He was focused on something to Galahir's right. Galahir followed his line of sight and his breath caught when he recognised Banahir's form standing away in the blackness, the distinct stag skull concealing his face.

A flicker of movement drew Galahir's attention back to the elf, and he was in time to see a cruel smile play over the thin lips as he raised a blowpipe to them, taking careful aim at Banahir. Before Galahir could raise a warning, the elf blew sharply into the pipe.

Banahir's cry of pain drowned out the noise of the forest, crumpling as something struck him in the midsection.

No! Without a thought to his own safety, Galahir sprinted forward towards his stricken clan brother. He caught Banahir before he could hit the ground. Blood was soaking the other man's furs and Galahir reached down, ripping a long, wicked looking barb from Banahir's belly.

He glared back into the trees, but he could no longer see the elf. He had disappeared. Even now, he could be fitting another barb into his blowpipe, readying to attack again. Heart in his mouth, Galahir swept Banahir from the ground and slung him across his shoulders before running as fast as he could back towards the safety of the camp. He did not know how many more of them could be hiding, readying to strike.

"What are you *doing* here?" he demanded of Banahir as he flew through the trees.

"S-searching for you." Banahir coughed. "I owed you after you saved me from that spider."

"You shouldn't have come," Galahir growled. Crushing guilt squeezed his chest. He had failed. The others had warned him that the elves had something planned, and he had not listened. Now Banahir had paid the price for his foolishness. He prayed the wound was not fatal. If Banahir died...

He should never have taken charge. Lorhir had been right about him. He was done trying to be a leader.

I'm sorry, Khalvir. I did all I could. I just wasn't enough.

***

CHAPTER 15

POWER

K halvir could no longer deny it. He had fallen in love with the elf witch who held him prisoner. And with that admittance came the knowledge that he had to find the strength to leave her, for her own good. It wasn't as if she loved him back. Not *him*, not Khalvir. It was this Juaan that she loved.

His heart contracted. He did not want her to see him as an enemy. He could not bear to lose that look of trust and love, no matter that it was meant for another, and see it replaced by resentment and hate. But what else was there? He thought again of what his Chief would do if this girl ever came into his clutches. Khalvir felt as if someone had closed their fist around his chest and squeezed. He would rather lose her regard than see her fall to such a fate.

He did not hear his men calling for him again, but that did not mean they had given up.

Utu rose in the sky as the clouds rolled overhead. Thoughtfully, Khalvir lifted the little leather pouch at his waist, weighing it in his hand. For the first time, he had the strangest urge to pull open the bindings and look inside, to see the contents he could feel beneath its smooth, supple skin. His fingers trembled at the opening, hesitating.

He dropped it quickly. He couldn't do it. He wasn't ready to discover the secrets of what lay within. Not yet.

The shadows were restless above him as the wind rustled in the trees. It was going to rain again. He could smell it. Khalvir groaned. He paced. Dozed. And then paced some more. The day wore on. He came to the unpleasant realisation that when one was trapped, rocks became so much more interesting.

He was bouncing pebbles against a chosen target on the far wall when a rustling overhead caught him by surprise. Khalvir shrank back against the stone wall, taking a defensive position. *She* never came during the day. He bent to pick up a large rock and waited.

"It's me," she whispered down, her face appearing above. He let out a breath and dropped the rock.

She slipped down into the pit, handing him the food she had brought. They settled into their customary positions as he ate the offering. She was quiet. For the first time he could see everything clearly in the revealing light of day; the exact shade of her skin, the draping, woven leaves covering her slight frame. The hollows of her cheeks cast harsh shadows. The skin under her eyes appeared bruised. She looked like she hadn't eaten or slept for days. Khalvir tightened his lips as the conviction that this situation must end hardened within his chest. It was killing her.

All of this he took in from the corner of his eye, not wanting to stare and make it apparent that he was studying her so closely. She, however, had no such reservations. She peered openly at him with tired eyes, almost hesitant, as though she had never really seen him before. A frown creased the skin at her brow. She did not appear at ease.

Khalvir felt a shiver of apprehension at the thought that she might finally be seeing him for who he was. He wasn't ready for that. Not yet.

He tried to keep his voice light as he asked. "What's the matter? You're looking at me as if I have two heads."

She shook herself. "Sorry."

"World on your shoulders?"

"I'm reassessing it," she murmured. "It's difficult."

"Ah." He swallowed the last bite with difficulty and waited for it to happen. She had finally come to see the truth about him. He could see the change in her eyes. "Anything to do with me?"

"Everything to do with you. You've caused me nothing but trouble."

He had. His lips pulled down. "Then let me go." *Let me go before I must hurt you.*

Hurt flashed through her eyes. He heard her soft intake of breath, and his heart sank. She was seeing him anew, but not yet clearly enough.

"I can't." Her voice trembled. She took a moment to compose herself. "I'm sorry," she said in a steadier tone. "I can't let you go. Not yet."

Khalvir looked up into the coverings above and sighed. Drips of cool rain were beginning to seep through the gaps and fall upon his upturned face. She was going to take this to the bitter end. He would have no choice but to hurt her. For her own sake.

"I wasn't expecting anything different, though it would be better for you if you did." His voice begged for her to heed his warning, to grasp the risk she was taking by keeping him here. Khalvir was amazed his men had not found him yet. Perhaps the wolves had given them pause in their search.

She came over and sat close beside him. He allowed it. The end was coming, and he would selfishly take everything he could get before that happened. That sense of completeness washed over him again, a balm to his soul. He closed his eyes, savouring the feeling.

"I can see your mother in you." The soft words came out of nowhere, soft like a velveted spear-head. They ripped through him, shattering his feeling of serenity. "She was of my tribe."

"I do not care who she was," Khalvir cut her off, struggling against his sudden anger. She had no right to pry. "And I do not want to know. I admit I may carry elf blood but not gladly, I am nothing of you."

"Yes, you *are.*" She was not going to back down this time. Determination glinted in her eyes. "You are more of us than them. I wish you could remember. I wish you could remember *me.*"

Khalvir remained silent, fighting with himself. He could not accept her words. He had to keep a hold on himself or he would bring about the end right now. The beast stretched inside him, flexing its claws.

Her frustration was palpable. "What do you remember?"

Khalvir was proud when he kept his voice sounding merely irritated. "I was found in a forest. My Chief told me an elf clan had been about to kill me. Elves do not believe in half-breeds. We are named Forbidden to all others. You say we are the evil ones, but your People would have put me to death simply for who I was. Because the so-called gods tell you that it should be so. That fact I have never forgotten."

He gave her a chilling glare. "Luckily we *Woves* have none of your superstitions. We know better. My clan took me in and nursed me back to health. When I was strong enough, I became *raknari,* a position of high honour. I protect my clan from those who would do them harm. That is all I know. All I *need* to know."

"No!" she denied. "That's not what happened. You were lost protecting me from being taken by the Woves. They were going to kill me but you would not let them." He could hear the emotion in her voice.

"We were only children. I thought they'd killed you. I thought I'd lost you forever, but now here you are and you remember nothing. Your mother—"

"Abandoned me," Khalvir growled, the pain of having her mentioned closing his throat. "She would never have kept a Forbidden child. She would've killed me. It's what witches do."

"No!" she hissed fiercely. "Your mother never abandoned you. She fought for you. She died keeping you alive through the long Fury. You owe her your life as I owe you mine."

"You owe me nothing," he growled. He got to his feet and walked away from her. She was hitting too deeply.

A gut-wrenching fear fuelled his anger; fear that what she said might be the truth. He could not make sense of these frightening sensations he could barely grasp. This need to be near her, the need to protect her.

Khalvir shook his head to clear it. To accept that would be to accept that his entire life had been a lie. These feelings of familiarity were nothing more than an effect of her power over him. He would not, could not, accept that what she told him was true.

He blocked out the shadows in his mind that fought to make themselves known. Lies, all of it. It wasn't real. "Say no more." He strained the words between his teeth. "I will not hear it." *Do not do this to me! I am Khalvir! I can't be who you think I am. I am not the one you love.* He felt his head would burst.

She let out a frustrated breath and relented. "Well, what shall we talk about, then?"

Khalvir took a few deep breaths, fighting to regain some semblance of composure. He spied something out of the corner of his eye. "That rock looks a bit like a wolf if you squint at it long enough," he said dryly.

She stared at him for a moment, then laughter bubbled from her throat. The sound chased away the last of Khalvir's demons. He realised he had never heard her laugh before, not freely or without bitterness. His love for her impossibly found new depths. "I'm glad my boredom amuses you," he grumbled without any real annoyance.

The rain started to fall harder. Khalvir sank back to the floor and huddled into his furs, resigning himself to yet another soaking.

She was watching him again. "Are your injuries bothering you?" she asked, her brow pinching together. "You look... uncomfortable."

His mouth twisted in dark amusement. "So would you if you'd been sleeping on bare rock for nights on end."

"But..." she seemed embarrassed to speak, "don't Woves usually sleep on the ground?"

Khalvir could not help but laugh at her childlike ignorance. "Yes, but not on the bare rock. We dark spirits need a few comforts, you know."

A flush crept up her cheeks as she glanced around the bare pit. After a few moments, she rose to her feet. He'd upset her. Khalvir felt a pang at the thought of her leaving already. But she only said, "I'll be right back," before scrambling out of the pit.

Khalvir waited as the rain drummed against the forest floor. Rivulets of water starting running down the back of his neck. He longed for proper shelter.

She was back before he had a chance to grow concerned. She threw down a large armful of leaves and a springy type of moss. He touched it with his fingers as it landed at his feet; it was very soft, like the fur of a rabbit. She disappeared and reappeared several times until she was satisfied with the amount of bedding that she had brought. Khalvir scraped it all into a pile close to one of the walls. Unfortunately, the overhang was only enough to prevent him from climbing out. It did nothing to block the rain.

"That should make things more comfortable for you," she called down from above. "But I'm afraid I have nothing for you to shelter under." She wiped a lock of dripping hair out of her face.

He raised an eyebrow at her. "But, you have all the materials you need." Khalvir couldn't resist taunting her a little, enjoying that he could play on her fierce pride. "Do you elves know nothing?" She opened her mouth to retort, but he waved a hand, dismissing her deliberately. "Find me some sturdy branches. I'll show you."

He did not let her see his amusement at the indigence in her eyes. Curiosity seemed to win her over, however, for she disappeared without further argument. She brought back a good selection of branches. This took a frustrating amount of time since she insisted on finding ones that had already fallen to the ground; she refused to take them from the trees. She reacted as if he had asked her to take her own arm off when he suggested it.

When she had at last brought back enough material and was standing in the pit with him once more, Khalvir set to work. He was showing off just a little. There was no need for this shelter to be so intricate, but he was feeling the need to impress; something he had never felt the need to do for a woman before. He was very pleased with the result. The shelter was small, but it was one of the best he had ever made.

He was rewarded by a look of reluctant amazement at his skill. She could not resist pointing out the obvious, however. "But there are still gaps in it. That's clever but you are still going to get wet." She sounded just a little smug.

"It's not finished yet," he growled defensively. "I need hides, but I won't get any of those around here, will I?" The elves didn't eat meat.

Khalvir highly doubted they knew how to cure skins; all they wore were leaves, and they were no sort of protection from the elements.

"No! You will not."

He chuckled once at the look of consternation on her face. "Don't worry. I wouldn't dare ask." He scrutinised her garments. At least they seemed to be handling the rain better than his. The water was sluicing right off the waterproof green leather rather than soaking into it. An idea struck. "Do you have any more of those leaves?"

She caught his train of thought almost immediately. A smile spread slowly across her face. "Wait here."

"Of course." He rolled his eyes.

It took her longer this time. Khalvir paced impatiently until she returned with a pile of thick leaves, as long and as broad as her arms. Perfect. "They'll do."

The problem remained, however, that he had nothing to attach them with. Khalvir draped one leaf experimentally over the wooden structure, but, large as it was, it was no deer skin. There wasn't enough of it to hang successfully in place. The slippery material simply slid to the ground as soon as he let go. "Hmmm."

There was a light touch on his arm. His skin prickled. He looked down and saw that her face was alight with excitement.

"I think I can solve that problem."

"How?"

"Don't you Woves know anything?" She smiled as she threw his words back at him. "Watch and I'll show you."

Now it was Khalvir's turn to be curious. He watched as her face grew blank with that now familiar expression of concentration. Moments later, a small, brightly coloured bird came and lighted on her waiting hand. She gazed intently at him, and he stared back with beady black eyes, cocking his head this way and that. She was *talking* to him,

Khalvir realised. And the bird understood. With a soft chirrup, he took off again.

"How are you doing that?" Khalvir tried to keep the wonder from his voice. He did not want to be impressed; elf magic had always been something to fear. From within and without. It prickled up his spine.

She smiled softly. "Ninmah's Gift. We are all family here. The Great Spirit binds us all. I told him what I needed and now he has gone to fetch it for me. Kyaati has a particular talent for birds." Her voice grew heavy at the last.

"Kyaati is the girl you are caring for?" he guessed gently, reading the pain on her face. "The girl who lost her baby?"

She nodded, her lips pressed tight.

"How—" Khalvir hesitated, unsure that she would want his concern. From her point of view, it was his clan's fault that her friend had been in the tree in the first place. "How is she recovering?"

"She isn't." Her voice was dead.

Khalvir was saved from a response by the return of the little bird. His eyes widened as the winged creature dropped a very large and rumpled spider onto the top of his wooden structure. The bird flitted away again and then returned, twice, each time with another dark brown crawler.

Upon bringing the third arachnid, the bird twittered around the girl. He landed on her shoulder and began pecking at her ear.

"Alright! Alright!" she cried, smiling, and held out a handful of plump seeds she had taken from her garments. The bird ate them quickly and then disappeared. Khalvir watched the amazing display before pulling his eyes away and shaking his head. "Elf magic," he muttered to himself.

She was not finished with her miracles, however. Now she focused on the spiders her bird had fetched for her. Her brow furrowed with the most intense look of concentration he had seen yet. The spiders sprang to life. They scurried over the shelter, leaving behind thick, sticky trails of silk. As they worked, so did she, placing her leaves ahead of the busy crawlers. The gleaming threads of silk bound the leaves in place, forming the desired skin over the skeleton of his shelter.

Khalvir marvelled at the sight.

At last she was finished. Her fine features relaxed, and she sank to the ground, apparently too exhausted to stand.

Unable to keep the wonder from his face, Khalvir circled the structure they had just made together. He had to work to keep his voice low and casual. "The first Wove-elf shelter ever made. It's... not bad." He looked sideways at her and allowed a smile to break onto his face. "Thank you."

She beamed at him, dispelling the drawn, haunted look that always seemed to cling to her, lighting up his world. Unbidden, they laughed together at the absurd situation that had found themselves in.

A blood-chilling snarl from above silenced them both. Nyri leaped to her feet, alarm flitting across her face. Khalvir spun around to face the threat, pushing the girl behind him.

He knew what he would find. He had heard such challenges many times before. The wolf's head was peering down into the pit, yellow eyes fixed upon him. Another snarl ripped from the beast's chest.

Instinctive fear rippled through him, but his life as a warrior tempered it as he reached automatically for a weapon. He knew it was a futile effort. Rocks would do no good here. But his mind continued to search for a solution as the wolf leaped down into the pit and stalked forward. Khalvir gritted his teeth.

"Batai?" she whispered to the beast, alarm in her voice. "Batai, stop. He's a friend."

"I don't think he's seeing it that way," Khalvir hissed between his teeth, taking on a defensive crouch as he backed slowly away from the advancing predator. There was no way he could win, but he would not go down without a fight.

"Batai! No!" she screamed as the wolf coiled and sprang.

Khalvir heard her frantic cry as though from a great distance. For a moment the world seemed to stop as Khalvir watched the wolf leap through the air, fangs aimed directly for his throat. He knew he was about to die. There was nothing he could do about that. He was a warrior; he was taught to accept death when it came, but did it have to be now, here, in this pit? With her watching?

Somehow, in that fraction of a moment, Khalvir caught her eye. He saw the horror, the fear, the heartbreak on her face. She should not see him die. He knew instinctively that it would break her.

Fury blazed within his soul, burning away the barriers to his centre. Released, the beast inside exploded forth, the strength of it terrifying as it tore loose. Gasping, Khalvir fought to control himself as he screamed. "Down, wolf!" and threw out his hands, preparing to block his enemy and protect his throat.

The blow of the heavy body never came. The wolf twisted in the air and landed in front of him. The creature looked as stunned as Khalvir felt. The powerful energy that had blazed through him evaporated, leaving him weak. His hands trembled.

There was silence. Nyri recovered first. She put her hands in the wolf's fur as if to comfort it. Khalvir was distantly aware that something was passing between them, and the wolf gave him one last look of contempt before it turned away with a huff and leaped up and out of the pit. A ringing starting somewhere in Khalvir's ears. He felt faint.

"What was *that*?" Her voice was stunned.

"I-I don't know," he mumbled, avoiding her eyes. "It happens sometimes. I can't control it." He paced away from Nyri. "This is the first time it has happened away from..." he trailed off. "Just consider yourself lucky you are still alive."

"This has happened before? Why didn't you tell me?"

"Why would I tell you," he shot at her. "It is nothing but a curse." The trembling moved from his hands, spreading through the rest of his body.

"It is no curse. You are half Ninkuraaja," the girl said. "You have your mother's blood. The Great Spirit of KI is within you." She paused. "I didn't think you possessed enough of Ninmah's Gift to control it. You struggled so much as a child. Somehow it came to you in that moment. You were in danger. Perhaps your body responded accordingly. Survival instinct."

Khalvir could not answer her. He felt sick. He coiled his fingers to stop them from shaking, turning to face the wall as he braced his arms against it. He drew in gulps of cold air. It had happened again. Fear shivered through him. It was lucky he had not—He screwed his eyes shut. He had yet again failed to control the monster inside. He could have killed her.

Khalvir listened through the buzz in his ears. Half expecting to hear her fleeing from him in terror. There was only silence. Then—

"Juaan." Her voice was soft and coaxing. "Juaan."

He turned his head slightly from the wall to meet her eyes. Why wasn't she frightened? One of her hands was extended. In the centre was a stone from one of the berries he had eaten. Her voice was still gentle as she continued. "Watch. Your abilities are nothing to be feared. I promise. I'll show you."

She focused her attention on the stone in her hand. Before Khalvir's eyes, the stone broke open and a tiny green shoot unfurled in the light, tasting its first kiss of the rain. It was beautiful. Khalvir could not help it. He moved away from the wall and came to stand before her. He bent his head over the stone. Such power, and she had used it to create *life*.

"How?" he whispered, hearing the tremor in his own voice.

Instead of answering, she reached out and caught his hand in her own, turning it palm up. She spilled the newborn plant onto his skin.

"Would you like me to teach you? You don't have to be afraid."

Don't have to be afraid? Khalvir felt a wave of longing. A longing of not having to fear the monster inside any more. His hand trembled anew as his desire and his deeply ingrained suspicions warred with one another. He looked into her deep, guileless eyes and the words were out of his mouth before he was even fully decided.

"Please, show me."

***

CHAPTER 16

SHUNNED

Galahir sat upon the fringes of the camp, miserable and alone. He still could not look the rest of the men in the eye as they continued to treat Banahir's injury. The puncture wound had been small but deep and very painful. It was only by the grace of the gods that it had not punctured anything vital.

One finger's breadth either way, and it could have been so much worse.

The other men did not speak to him. They muttered among themselves, casting dark glances. Some did this when they thought he was not looking. Others, like Ranab, did so boldly, glaring at the witless half-Thal who had dared to try to lead them and almost getting one of their number killed in the process.

Galahir kept his head down. All he had wanted to do was to save his clan brother, and he had failed in that, too. He gazed broodingly into the trees. Somehow, even after everything, his heart was telling him that Khalvir was still alive in there somewhere. He just didn't understand why his brother had ceased to answer his calls.

Galahir got up and paced restlessly, feeling trapped. There was no way he could enter the forest again. He had used up all of his chances.

Next to the fire, Banahir let out a loud moan. Unable to help himself, Galahir rushed towards his fellow warrior.

"Banahir? Are-?"

Immediately, three of the other men blocked his view of Banahir as the stricken man doubled up over his wound.

"You have no right to go near him, Galahir," Ranab spat, his eyes burning, fuelled by the fear for his sibling. "This is *your* fault. We warned you and you ignored us. Stay away from him, we will take care of your mistake, *halfwit*."

Galahir's pale cheeks flamed, but he could think of nothing to say in his defence. He turned away, intent on returning to his isolation.

A snigger sounded behind him. "No reaction, eh? A real warrior would not allow such an insult to his honour. You never were any more than Khalvir's tamed *beast*."

A distinctive whistle was Galahir's only warning, and he swept his hand up just in time to catch Ranab's *arshu* as it came whistling towards his back. The blow hadn't aimed to be fatal, merely to sting, but the attack from a brother-in-arms hurt, nevertheless.

Ranab's face twisted as he tried to wrench his weapon out of Galahir's grasp. He could not move it so much as a fraction. He snarled in frustration. The men surrounding them shifted uneasily, unsure of what to do.

Galahir sighed and lifted the weapon that Ranab was still fighting to free from his grip, hoisting the other man off the ground as he did so. "I do not want to hurt you, Ranab, so leave it be. I cannot be more sorry that Banahir got hurt than I already am. I never meant for it to happen." He flexed his arm, swinging Ranab's *arshu,* and then let go. Ranab fell to earth in a heap. "Just... leave me be."

With that, he turned and walked away, hearing nothing but the furious silence behind him.

For the first time in his life, Galahir longed for Lorhir's return.

**

CHAPTER 17

UNCONTROLLABLE

The next time Nyri appeared, her eyes held the sadness of death. Khalvir guessed that if it wasn't for the darkness, he would see that the skin around her eyes was red and raw, like her voice. Something terrible had happened while she had been away.

Her grief was such that Khalvir was almost afraid to ask, and when she refused to share her pain the first time; he did not pry further. Instead, he distracted her. He wanted to learn how to control the beast inside him. She latched on to the opportunity to forget her troubles gratefully.

As the days passed, Khalvir almost wished he had refused her offer. Nothing of his *raknari* training could compare to the difficulty of what she was trying to teach him. He could feel the power within, but trying to control it was like trying to grasp water.

It was a great shadow, bodiless, dancing away from his touch. He lost his temper more than once, but Khalvir found it was only when he was angry that he could call the power forth. The results of these instances were not what either of them had hoped for. His energy only seemed to have the power to destroy; he could not make a seedling grow. If she brought anything living for him to practice with, his raw power rushed forth to overwhelm and kill it. Khalvir was grateful that she had only ever brought him plants.

Though Khalvir was not progressing as either of them had hoped, as the time passed, he was finding it easier to sense the world around him, feeling its vibrations more readily against his senses. But the ability to make a seed grow was still beyond him. A blackened pile of his failed attempts littered the ground of the pit.

Though alarmed by his destructive ability, the girl remained supportive and patient. Often she would lay a hand on his arm and merge her will with his. It was only then he truly understood, almost saw everything she described, and a sense of peace fell over him. It was not a serenity he ever thought to find while being held captive in the bottom of a hole in the company of an elven woman. Nyriaana.

She stirred his very soul. Khalvir felt he could live out his whole life in this hole if he could just be with her. While she was with him, everything else melted away.

When she was gone, it was a different story. Despite his new comfortable shelter, Khalvir could not rest. His men had still not returned, and their absence now worried him more than their calls. He did not know where they might be. He worried they had given up their search and were instead hunting; hunting for the elves. They would not go back to their Chief empty handed. Khalvir did not sleep.

He was restlessly preparing to face down another long, sleepless day when the leaves above drew back with a soft rustle. And there she was.

He could not let her see the pleasure her presence brought him. "A day time visit," he said offhandedly. "I am honoured."

"You should be." She replied in the same tone. "I'm a busy elf."

Khalvir hid his smile. Then he took in her appearance. She was far worse than the last time he had seen her in the light. Fear for her twisted in his chest. "You look exhausted. You should take time to rest. You are not getting enough."

She rubbed her eyes, a sharp frown showing that his words were not welcome. "I wonder whose fault that is?" she snapped.

He ignored her flare of temper. "Yours. I'm not keeping myself down here, you know."

She growled and thrust out the food she had brought as she sat. He smiled, knowing he had won this time, and ate hungrily.

Khalvir watched her from the corner of his eye, as he always did. Her eyes had fallen closed, her head leaning wearily back against the stone wall. She couldn't have been comfortable, but the relief was clear on her face. He was glad she was finally resting. Lessons could wait today. But as Khalvir looked more closely, he could see the peace was tortured. The frown remained fixed between her brows, the skin around her eyes was tight and marked by layers of dried tears. She appeared to be listening to something and did not like what she heard.

Khalvir moved closer to her. He longed to be able to remove the pain from her face. "What is it?" he asked softly.

Her eyes opened. She looked far older than when they had first met. "Ninsiku approaches in all his Fury and the world trembles," she whispered.

"You mean the winter?"

She nodded. "Yes. Can't you feel it? Every cycle, I feel him approach, but this time, this time…" she hunched her wiry shoulders protectively. "I fear it. It feels like the beginning of the end."

Khalvir raised his hand to the air. It was cold, colder than it should be for this season. He could feel the changes. Experience told him the winter would be harsh. "Hmmm," he agreed. "It will be a long and cruel one. I fear you are right."

A soft whine sounded from overhead and Khalvir looked up to see a large furry head peering down at them. The wolf had become a constant companion of late. Its presence made Khalvir less than comfortable, though the beast had made no further attempts on his life.

The wolf met his gaze and flattened his pointed ears against his grey head as he curled a lip.

"He still does not like me," he said.

Nyri was unperturbed. "Maybe because you wear his dead kin about your body," came her pointed response. Disgust twisted her face as she eyed his coverings. She was in a sour mood today.

"Sorry," was all he could think to say. "It's not personal, simply a matter of survival." Khalvir eyed her clothing right back. "I can't imagine that those leaves offer you much protection." She was almost always shivering.

Her lips pulled down as her face contracted. He wished he hadn't spoken. Khalvir held out the last of his ration to her. "Take it. You look as if a gust of wind would blow you away."

He knew how hungry she must be when she took his offering with no more protest than a grateful smile. He wondered if she was eating at all when she was away from him. He did not care for the thought.

Her eyes remained distant as she chewed and Khalvir knew she had not admitted to the core reason for her brooding. "What else concerns you? It is not just the coming of the winter."

She looked up at him with a quizzical frown. "I thought you said you didn't know me?"

He shrugged. Sometimes he felt like he could read her face as though he had known it his entire life.

She sighed and admitted, "It's Kyaati. She is ill and not getting any better. I do not know how to reach her. I fear," her breath caught as tears started in her eyes. "I fear we are going to lose her, too."

Khalvir's arms twitched towards her. He thought to the first night he had seen her and of how, even then, she had stirred his soul with her fierce determination. He would not see that spirit lost.

"Do not give up. You will find a way." He dared to reach out and brush her hand with his fingers. "I remember the night she fell. You flew down like a falcon and tried to beat me with a stick to save her." He smiled softly as he admitted. "I noted your bravery even then. If you can do that and if she has even half your courage, she will recover."

She blinked at him, shocked by his admittance. Khalvir could not hold her gaze lest he reveal too much. He kept his eyes fixed upon the wolf. There was something he wanted to know, though he dreaded the answer. "Did the fall...? Was it our fault?" He struggled to make himself clear.

She understood. "No." She blew out the word. "I wanted to blame you. I wanted it to be the Woves' fault, but it was not. The baby was born malformed. Whether Kyaati had fallen from that tree or not, the result would have been the same." Her voice grew distant. "It is happening more and more frequently, our children born dead or deformed. We have always believed that you," she waved a hand at him, "Woves were the cause of our growing weakness, cursing us with some black magic that we could not understand. I was so certain.... But you do not have that power, do you?" Her face was bitter.

"I'm afraid not," he said. "Only what I've picked up from your People, it seems." Khalvir turned what she had told him over in his head. The elves were dying out. Only fifteen in her tribe, she had told him, a lifetime ago now it seemed. He could guess what was happening. The Cro had once faced such a fate, but they had been smart enough to forsake the gods' tenets, unlike the others who still so stubbornly clung to such teachings. The elves had doomed themselves. And they could not see it.

"Well, whatever the cause." Her voice pulled Khalvir from his thoughts. "We are dying. Soon there won't be any of us left for the Woves to hunt." She fixed him with a searching stare. "Why do you hunt us? You never told me. If the Woves don't eat us and do not serve Ninsiku in his vendetta to see us dead, why do they come?"

Khalvir debated whether or not to speak, to tell her it was the power of healing, of life over death, that had caused his Chief to hunt her kind for all this time, and that she possessed the very power that drew death to her People.

He had not yet made up his mind to speak when she turned sharply, distracted by something beyond his senses. He followed her gaze. The wolf had disappeared. "What is it?"

"Deer," she murmured. "There is a small herd browsing away in the trees, downwind from Batai. The breeze just carried their scent to him. He's hungry. He has scarcely left Omaal's side apart from to accompany me here at night."

"Omaal?" This was a new name.

"One of the children." She quickly explained the bond between the wolf above and a blind boy in her tribe, about how they were so closely bonded, the boy could use the wolf's sight to navigate. Khalvir listened with disbelief and not a little envy. The wolves may be enemies to his clan and rivals in the hunt, but they were a predator without rival and he admired their skill. To be able to join with such creatures, to become partners in the hunt... He shook his head. "I wonder what it is like to see through a wolf's eyes?"

"Do you want to try?"

Khalvir took a step back. "I can do that?"

"I don't see why not."

"What if I harm him?" This creature was no expendable seed upon which to test his unpredictable powers. Khalvir knew she would never forgive him if he killed the wolf.

"You won't. I have faith in you." Nyri took his wrist. Khalvir tensed at her touch, feeling his skin prickle. It wasn't only the power radiating from her that caused it. Heat trickled down his back at the very feel of her. "Focus. I will guide you."

Focus. He fought to bend his will to the task and close out all other sensations. Her fingers on his arm were almost making it impossible. Khalvir clenched his teeth.

The energy was there. Deep inside him it resided, like a ravening wolf itself, just waiting to be released. He struggled as always to catch it, his fear of what it might do hindering him still further. Then suddenly Nyriaana was there. Her energy was bright inside him and it bridged the connection between him and his own.

Khalvir stretched forth eagerly, and she went with him, guiding him to where he needed to go, tempering his own wild and ravenous Gift. Life blazed all around. It was hard to focus on any one thing. He could feel everything with a dizzying intensity. If it wasn't for his guide, he would have been lost.

Under her careful guidance, Khalvir merged with the wolf's consciousness. The experience was odd. Both he and the wolf occupied the same space, one body, two minds, but, as he grew accustomed, the sensation was beyond anything he could have ever imagined.

His every sense sharpened; hearing, smell, the feel of the ground under his paws. The scent... Khalvir could *smell* the deer through the wolf's nose. Then the images came, images of the feast, of tender juices filling his mouth and slacking his hunger. Khalvir realised he was seeing the wolf's own wordless thoughts. Khalvir's own hunger rose in answer, a hunger that fruit and roots alone could not satisfy. He wanted to hunt!

His sudden desire fanned the power inside him, bursting it into flames. His energy surged forth, overtaking Nyriaana's guidance, unleashing itself on the wolf's conscience.

No! Khalvir tried to pull back, fearing the animal's mind would be consumed by his power. The wolf's own thoughts vanished before the onslaught and he suddenly found himself alone inside this foreign head. His own thoughts occupied the entire space. *He* was the wolf now, not simply a passenger.

His mind whirled, disorientated, but then the smell of the deer became too much to bear, and animal instinct overrode his thoughts. A howl found its way past lips that were not his own. His new body bunched and shot forward as he charged towards the deer. The sensation of running on all fours threw him for one moment, but then Khalvir caught his stride. The disorientation evaporated, and he found himself revelling in the speed and the sensation; the stretch and pull of his powerful muscles as he bore down swiftly upon his prey.

But Khalvir did not know how to hunt as a wolf. His first strike was clumsy and ill timed. The herd broke apart. He hared after them, thinking of nothing but running them down. The deer turned and began thundering headlong back towards the pit. The ground shook as the panicked animals broke around the rocky edges, sharp hooves scrambling to keep from falling in. He was close, so close to sinking his teeth into a straggler's hindquarters—

A terrible, ripping, crumbling sound broke Khalvir's concentration. His senses snapped dizzyingly back into his own body and he heard a confused yelp above him as the wolf returned to its own mind. Someone was screaming inside his head. He blinked his own human eyes open, and they widened in shock as he took in the horrifying scene that was playing out before him.

The deer that he had chased into the path of the pit had dislodged a massive rock from the crumbling edges. The rock was tumbling, cracking against the wall as it fell, straight down towards—

"Nyriaana!" Her name ripped from his chest. She was standing frozen, watching in detached horror as her death tumbled towards her.

No!

Khalvir did not stop to think. He threw himself forward, knocking her small body out of the way of the tumbling rock.

Midair, he twisted over so he wouldn't land with his full weight on top of her. As his body slammed into the ground, he felt something hard and sharp rip through his furs and gouge deep into his right shoulder. A cry escaped his lips as he rolled again, putting her beneath his own body and shielding her head with his arms as the boulder smashed into the ground behind them with a resounding crack. Birds in the trees above took to the air, shrieking in panic.

Silence. Khalvir could feel every part of her body trembling against his. He couldn't move. The pain in his shoulder throbbed with the rhythm of his blood. He could hear it rushing in his ears. His vision blurred as he gated the groan between his teeth.

"Juaan." Her voice was a breath. She struggled out of his hold. "Juaan." Freeing herself, she stood, and Khalvir heard her suck in a breath as he forced himself to sit upright, dislodging pebbles and other debris scattered across the rock behind him. A jagged branch lay not far away. A sharp protrusion was red with his blood. Khalvir reached back to assess the damage. The wound was deep. His hand came back dripping. He raised an eyebrow at it. Yet another scar.

"Who's there!" A male voice called out from above. An elf voice. Beside him, Nyriaana froze, her skin draining of all colour. Her tribe had heard the commotion, and they were coming to investigate. Men who would attack him on sight.

Khalvir's heart sank. He was going to be forced to fight and kill Nyriaana's own kin in front of her. She would see the monster she had blinded herself to at last.

Before he could brood over this unfortunate turn of events, she was moving, springing forward, and wrapping her body tightly around his own. The sudden movement startled him. Khalvir protested, afraid of her proximity, afraid of the part of himself that liked it. His shoulder screamed as she jostled it.

"Be still!" she hissed her warning. "I've got to hide us. They'll kill you!"

Khalvir stopped struggling against her grip and grew still, half in readiness for his enemy's appearance, half in curiosity as to what she was trying to do.

Then he felt it. Days of her teaching had honed the senses that he had long suppressed. Her energy gathered around them, like a fur cocooning them in its warmth. The sense of power increased. The hairs prickled on the back of Khalvir's neck as her essence imbued itself with his own.

He could *feel* her, not just physically. It was as if they shared every breath and every heartbeat as their energies merged. Khalvir was frozen in awe and in terror. Never had he imagined it was possible to feel so close to anyone. He wanted to escape, but he could not. He could feel her drawing on his own energy. It wanted to respond, but he controlled it, unsure of the mess it might make. Her body was faintly trembling from the effort. Khalvir still had no clue as to what she was doing.

A face appeared above them, peering into the pit. A thin male face framed by straight black hair with smooth red-gold skin drawn into a frown. Pale purple eyes scoured every detail of his surroundings.

Khalvir tensed, fingers finding a fist sized rock next to his hand, readying to dispatch his enemy with one flick of his wrist as soon as he came within range. It wasn't just his life in the balance now. He knew in being found with him, Nyriaana's life would also be forfeited. That was something he could not allow. The elf above would have to die. He hoped she would come to forgive him.

No! The reprimand was loud in his head, startling him. *Don't hurt him!*

The eyes swept closer to where they huddled. Khalvir's hand tightened upon his rock, ready to ignore her command... And they passed right by. Khalvir stared in disbelief. The elf had looked right at them and moved on. No, Khalvir corrected his thought. He had looked right *through* them, as if they were not present. Nyriaana had made them invisible to her tribesmen. There was no end to the wonders of elf magic.

Khalvir watched, remaining on guard until the watchman turned and moved away. Long moments passed, filled only with the sound of their joined breaths. They were no longer in danger, but she did not let him go. He did not want her to, but that thought alone made him move, breaking out of her death hold. "I think he's gone. You can let go now." Khalvir could hear the strain in his own voice as he tried to control his emotion. The feeling of being bound to her had been too great. She was part of him now, a piece of her soul forever attached to his.

"Are you all right?" her voice was tight.

"I think so," he said, carefully. He rubbed the back of his head, trying to remember himself. "Are you unharmed?"

Her response came in one of those waves of fury that always took him by surprise.

"Of course I am!" she snapped. "You knocked me out of the way." She was so mad she was almost choking on her rage. "You fool, you could've been killed! They could have found us! How many times have I told you what it would do to me to lose you again!" A couple of tears spilled down her cheeks. She was obviously fighting against breaking down entirely. Khalvir could tell that she was reaching her limit. She was under too much strain.

"Easy," he soothed. "You're in shock."

"Of course I am!" she snarled. "I nearly died. Again. They nearly found *you*!"

Khalvir felt like she had punched him in the gut. He had lost count of how many times she had risked her life for him. His face clouded at the thought of this latest near miss. They could not go on like this. It had already gone on too long.

Nyriaana seemed to catch his expression. She closed her eyes and took a few deep, calming breaths. "I'm sorry," she said after a few moments. Slowly, she moved to kneel in front of him. She looked at the blood dripping onto the rock. "Will you let me heal you?" she asked. She read the hesitation in his eyes and persisted. "Please. I need to see that there is no serious damage. If a rock struck your head..." Her fists clenched.

Khalvir was torn. It wasn't that he didn't trust her now. But the thought of being so close to her was frightening him more and more. He had to let go, and she was only making it harder.

Her eyes pleaded with him, hurt at what she saw as his continued rejection and raw with the need to take care of his wellbeing. Khalvir's will crumbled. He could not deny her. "If you wish."

"Thank you." Her face filled with gratitude. She moved around him, studying the damage to his shoulder. "I need you to take these off."

Khalvir had not foreseen this. If he removed his coverings, there were things he knew she would see that he would rather she did not. He knew her well enough by now to predict her reaction.

"Please." She pushed. "I need to see."

Gritting his teeth, Khalvir pulled the furs from his back. The cold stung at his skin and he restrained a shiver.

From the corner of his eye, he watched as an embarrassed flush crept up her cheeks and she ducked her head away. For the first time, he felt oddly vulnerable in his nakedness. He wanted to hide from her. He kept his eyes studiously on the far pit wall as a soft, horrified gasp told him he had been right in his prediction. She had seen.

The need to heal his wound deflected an immediate response, but he could feel the brewing emotions in her touch even as the pain in his shoulder receded. She was gathering like a storm on the horizon, and Khalvir braced for the impact as she finished her task. Then his own temper stirred. He shouldn't be dreading her reaction. She had no right to judge.

"What in Ninmah's name *happened* to you?" The storm broke. She moved to the front of him, where he could see clearly the anger and pain in her eyes. "What did they do to you?" Her hand reached out to touch the long scar on his shoulder. He subtly shifted out of her reach, and she dropped her hand. "Tell me."

"It is not for you to know." He did not have to tell her anything.

"Don't give me that," she growled, once again surprising him with her audacity. He was not used to being challenged so. "Tell me. Where have all these scars come from? Who did this to you?"

Khalvir tightened his jaw in frustration. Her only response was to sit down in front of him, making it clear she would not leave until he spoke. "Please."

He let out a long, silent breath through his nose, fighting to keep his patience. "You would not understand, elf."

"Help me understand," she pleaded. "I want to help you."

Sadness swept through him in the face of her innocence. "It is nothing you can fix. Nothing has been *done* to me but life." He drew a deep breath. He yearned to share a small part of himself with her, to have somebody see him and accept what he was. Thinking carefully about his words, Khalvir began. "When my clan found me, it surprised them to find that I was half elf—"

"There are no other Forbidden Ninkuraaja in your clan?" she interrupted, eyebrows raised.

"No. I am the only one. My clan Chief hoped I would possess the power of my elf witch heritage. When it became clear that I could not control it, he was... disappointed. I had to be found another use." He omitted the first use his Chief had put him to. She would turn from him if he did. He would allow her to see only a part of the monster. "When he witnessed me defeat another clan member in a brawl, he gave me over to the spear master to become *raknari.*"

"What is *raknari*?"

"A warrior," he explained. "We are trained to protect the clan from any threat, to do anything it takes, no matter the consequence, the survival of the clan is all."

"No matter the consequence? They would expect you to die for the clan?"

Khalvir nodded stiffly, annoyed by her tone of consternation and lack of understanding. To die for the clan was the least of it. "It is a great honour to be *raknari* and to protect one's clan."

"How do you become *raknari*?

Khalvir shrugged evasively. Some memories were too painful to share. "It is not easy."

"Tell me."

"Training is hard and very few survive the *raknari* life for long. You win or you die."

"Few *survive*?" Her face was aghast. "I assume by that you mean you fight one another. Other tribes?"

"*Yes*," he hissed, losing patience. She was prying too deeply into wounds that had only ever scabbed over and could never fully heal. The slightest reminder had them bleeding again. Khalvir gritted his teeth. "Only the strongest survive to become *raknari*. Only the strongest survive *life*. Good territories are getting harder to come by. To secure one, we must be prepared to fight for it and then defend it by any means necessary."

Khalvir watched as Nyriaana turned her face away from him to stare determinedly at the cold, grey wall of the Pit. Her jaw worked. She was trying to contain whatever emotion was struggling to break loose. She must be disgusted with him, and Khalvir waited for her to leave.

Tears slid silently down her cheeks. After a long, tense moment, she turned her large eyes upon him, looking right into his soul. Khalvir was caught off guard. There was no censure in her gaze, only sorrow. "They hurt you." Her voice was a breath, meaning so much more than just the physical wounds.

He reached out to touch her cheek, amazed by her tears. "You weep for me?" No one had ever wept for him before. Much less some-one who should be his enemy. He was *raknari*. He was expendable. "Why?"

Frustration burned in her eyes as if his density was forcing her to admit something she shouldn't have to say aloud. "Can you not figure it out?" she hissed, wiping her eyes. "Have I not made it perfectly clear? I love you, Juaan. I always have. I cannot bear to see you hurt. Even to protect me."

Khalvir's breath caught in his chest. He wasn't even sure if his heart was still beating. She might have called him by another's name, but that did not matter. She had been looking right into his soul when she spoke. His. And he did not know how to respond.

He could not admit his feelings for her. It would destroy them both when the inevitable happened. And that must happen soon. He watched her as she bowed her head, hiding her eyes from him. She looked so sad, so vulnerable in her admittance.

He reached out to touch her smooth cheek, unsure, hesitant. He would admit one thing to her, one truth. "I... could not see you hurt, either."

Her eyes came up, hopeful, and that nameless feeling swelled until Khalvir could barely contain it. The flashes of half seen images and emotion flickered in the shadows of his mind. Something, something he should know. It taunted him with its closeness. He shuddered, pulling his hand back. "What is it about you, elf? I do not know." Khalvir looked deep into her eyes, fighting, wanting to understand, to know, but the images fled, dancing just out of his grasp.

Nyriaana reached out and caught his hands between her own before he could retreat. He closed his eyes briefly at the feel of her fingers on his.

"Please stay with me, Juaan," she whispered. "You do not have to go back there. I cannot let you go back. You are not their killer. They took you from me, now come back."

Yes! I'll stay with you. He wanted to say it. Khalvir wanted to remain in this moment forever, but she must know as well as he that it was not possible. A bitter smile twisted his face.

"How?" he asked. "Even if I wanted to, even if what you are saying is true and I am a boy you knew long ago, how can I stay here? My life with my clan may be hard but your People," he pointed to the place where the watchman had stood only a short time ago as he stared her full in the face, "would kill me."

She knew the truth. He could see it in her eyes. She wanted desperately to deny it, to cling on to an imagined dream, but she could not. More tears started in her eyes as she dropped his hands and turned away.

CHAPTER 18

PAIN

The buzzing of insects was becoming unbearable. The flying menaces were braving the cold, drawn out by the promise of drying blood on his skin and furs. Khalvir moved to put the garments back on, to block them from tickling his back.

"You can't put those on," she admonished him. The need for action seemed to shake her from the depression she had fallen into. "I'm going to have to take them and wash them in the river." A spasm of concern pinched her face as she gazed up at the deepening sky.

The break in the tension was a relief. Khalvir brooded. She had to go, and he needed to think. He needed to decide. "Make sure you bring them back," he said gruffly, folding his arms against the chill. He was already missing their protection.

He was rewarded with a soft smile. "I will. They needed a wash anyway. You were beginning to stink." She wrinkled her nose dramatically as she lifted the dark furs.

Khalvir rolled his eyes at her comment and lifted his eyebrows as he spread his arms to indicate the lack of open water in the prison she kept him in.

"I know, I know," she muttered in response, her attention already on the rope that would carry her to the surface. She struggled under the weight of his furs and a frown crumpled her brow as she tilted her head to judge the climb.

Despite himself, Khalvir fought the grin that was threatening to break out and only partially succeeded. "Here." He took the garments from her, swung back his arm, and launched them up and over the edge.

She was watching him with her mouth hanging slightly open. The flush crept back up her cheeks and she ducked her head. "Show off," she muttered as she took hold of the rope and hauled herself up and out of sight.

Khalvir let the smile drop from his face as soon as she disappeared, sinking down against the rock wall. He flinched as his back contacted the icy stone and huddled down over his knees, closing his eyes.

I love you, Juaan. I always have.

No one had ever loved him, not in the way she looked at him. He shivered as he remembered her face as she had spoken the words. The feel of her skin against his fingers.

I always have.

Khalvir screwed his eyes shut.

Please stay with me...

He groaned into his knees.

He did not know for how long he had dozed when a heavy thud beside him shocked him awake. Before his eyes were fully open, his body reacted to the threat. Khalvir's arm shot out, fingers closing around the throat of the intruder as he threw them to the ground.

"Juaan," the familiar voice croaked through his choke hold.

His fingers released her like they had been burned. "How many times?" he swore. "Don't surpri—" And then he saw her fully and the last vestiges of sleep evaporated. She remained crumpled upon the ground, her breath coming in sporadic hitches. The broken expression on her face was terrible to behold. "What's wrong?" he demanded. "Did I hurt you?" He could have broken her chest with the force of his attack.

"No." She shook her head. "But nothing will be ever right again!" She broke down, burying her face in her hands to stifle her uncontrolled sobs. "What have I *done*?"

Khalvir had never seen her like this. Something red caught his eye. "You're bleeding!" The skin on the inside of her right arm had been cut open. Blood was oozing from the wound, sliding down her skin to drip onto the ground. He was at her side before he even really thought about it, putting his hand around her arm to examine the wound.

He knew what had made such a cut. The edges of the wound were clean, not ripped and jagged as they would have been if she had simply caught herself on a branch or been bitten by an animal. "What *happened*?" he demanded, fighting the urge to shake her. If one of his men—

"Daajir," she choked out. "We argued. I-I hit him and he cut me with your knife."

Daajir. A red haze descended over Khalvir's vision. Fury burned through him at the sound of the unfamiliar name. One of her own had done this. His hand tightened upon her arm. "*Why*?" He barely recognised his own voice as it slid between his teeth. He was shaking. In this moment, he could not remember ever being so furious. This *Daajir*, the name burned through him again, had attacked her. Khalvir would kill him for that. His hand itched towards his waist and the knife that was no longer there.

"He wants to do something, something terrible. He's created a poison. He wants to use it on you. On the Woves. But I can't let him. I can't let him. If he finds *you*..."

Khalvir broke away from her. "He better hope *I* do not find *him*." If this Daajir wanted a fight, he would give him one. He would suffer for this unforgivable crime. Khalvir would throw him into the gods' damnation. He started for the rope. The rest of her tribe may overpower him. He did not care so long as he found Daajir first.

"No!" Nyriaana grabbed his arm. "Stay with me. I need you, Juaan. I need you now. Please. Stay. I need..."

Her pleading broke over his fury like a cascade of water, dowsing it. The red haze drained from Khalvir's vision as he turned his gaze to her desperate face. The rope beckoned, offering him a path to vengeance, but she held him as surely as if he were bound to the rock. He could not leave her.

Khalvir shuddered and sank to the ground a little distance away. "What do you need?"

Before he could react, Nyriaana threw herself at him and curled into his side. He was quite unable to breathe. Khalvir was sure he was trembling just as much as she was. He should pull away. He could not *do* this.

"Please," she begged, as if reading his thoughts. Her eyes slid closed as she pulled herself closer. Warmth engulfed his heart. Before he could question himself, his arm was winding around her shoulders, holding her as he had dreamed of doing for so long now. His body quivered as she turned her face into the side of his chest and nuzzled his bare skin. "Just... speak to me."

"About what?" He could barely get the words out.

"Anything."

"You realise you forgot my furs," he murmured, unable to think of anything better to say. It did not matter. She was already gone, overcome at last by her exhaustion. Her soft, even breaths tickled the hairs across his chest. Khalvir melted into her. He should wake her, but he could not bring himself to do so. He would let her remain for a while, to rest out of danger. Lowering his face, he pressed his lips into her dark hair.

One more night, just one more night, and then he would let her go.

The cold of the night began to make itself known. Khalvir gathered her delicate body into his arms and carried her into the embrace of his little shelter. They would be more comfortable inside with the moss to protect them from the biting ground. He laid her down on the soft bedding; she was so exhausted, she did not even stir. Khalvir sat beside her. In sleep, her face appeared even younger, more innocent. He reached out with his fingers to stroke her cheek. *I'm so sorry,* he thought, *I'm so sorry for what we have done to you. I won't put you in danger any longer. I will keep them away, even if it costs me my own life.* He would take no witches back to his Chief. He just had to be certain she was not here when his men came. If they saw her, he would be powerless.

"Juaan," she murmured in her sleep. "Don't leave me."

With a helpless groan, Khalvir wrapped his body around hers, wishing he could hold her there forever. Her warmth spread through his body as her soft breaths lulled him. *Just one more night.* He vowed he would not be here beside her when she awoke, but for now, he could not fight what he was feeling. Khalvir buried his face in her hair, inhaling her familiar scent as sleep dragged him under...

Something was moving under his arm, but Khalvir felt no alarm, as he might otherwise have done. He was at peace. He breathed deeply in contentment, tightening his hold on his possession. The light of dawn pressed pleasantly against his eyelids as he slid back towards sleep.

His arm tugged again, and reluctantly he opened his eyes.

Her face was right there, indigo eyes wide with surprise. *No!* Dismay rippled through him. It was morning, and he was still wrapped firmly around her. Khalvir rolled loose, furious at himself for his lack of control. This had gone far enough, farther than he had ever meant to go. He was weak and his weakness was going to cost Nyriaana her life.

"I'm sorry," he mumbled. "I-it was cold, and you didn't bring my furs back."

With his newly awakened senses, Khalvir felt a flash of hurt. He was hurting her by his cool disregard, but this hurt was nothing compared to the hurt that was coming.

He kept his back to her so that she wouldn't see the agony on his face as he made his decision. It was time. He could no longer let his weakness rule him. He had to break the connection. Her love for him would only end in her destruction.

As if to vindicate his thoughts, a whistle pierced the air in the distance. His men were coming. It had to end.

"Juaan."

No. He could not be her Juaan. He was Khalvir, her enemy. That was all there was, all there could be.

"Juaan...?" He felt her fingers brush his arm.

No!

If he let her touch him, he could not do what he needed to. He flinched away. "No! No more. I can't allow it. I am *Khalvir*. I am not your Juaan. I cannot be who you think I am. I should not have allowed you to keep coming to me. It would have been better for the both of us if you had just killed me from the start." He crawled from the shelter.

He was suddenly furious, raging against the pain in his heart. This was all her fault. Why had she had to come into his life and made him suffer like this?

Khalvir tensed as she followed him. "Juaan, don't. Don't do this to me! Please, not now. I need you. Why are you saying these things?"

Her tears threatened to break his resolve. Khalvir hardened his heart and tried to block out the sound of her sobs.

"Just *leave*. Go back to your People where you belong."

A hysterical laugh burst from her, catching Khalvir by surprise. He risked turning to look at her face. Her expression was almost more than he could bear. "I'm not sure if I do anymore. I struck another Ninkuraa. Such a crime is forbidden." She turned her eyes on him, beseeching. "Please, Juaan, Juaan listen to me. Your clan is still here. They have been searching for you."

Yes, I know, and you need to get out of here. Now!

She swallowed in the face of his stony expression, seeming to screw up her courage. Then, in a small voice, she asked. "You are their leader. You can save the lives of my People and your own. You must order them away. Tell them to leave. If you can make my People safe, I-I will leave. I needn't see you again."

Shock ricocheted through Khalvir. There it was, the true motive he had been waiting for. The betrayal stung worse than he had ever imagined. She wasn't here just for him, as he had foolishly begun to believe. "So that's it?" He laughed to hide the hurt. "That is why you have been coming here? You thought you could use me to order my People away from your forest?" He laughed again. She had fooled him so completely, made him feel like someone like him could be loved. All she had really wanted was to worm her way into his affections and turn him on his own to save hers. Her leaders had no doubt sent her here. It had all been a ruse. Khalvir knew it was irrational to feel so much anger at something he had secretly expected all along, but he couldn't help himself. He was in too much pain.

The witch was shaking her head, still trying to maintain the lie as she reached for him. "No, no, that is not the only reason, I have not lied. I love you, Juaan."

"No more. No more lies." He turned away in disgust. It was time for his own truth. "You have wasted your time, witch. I cannot do what you say. I cannot order my men away."

"Why *not*?" Her face crumpled, as if he had taken the last shred of hope from her.

Khalvir threw his hands up. "Because they will never stop coming, you fool! I am not their true leader. My clan Chief will not stop until he gets what he wants."

"Your chief?" Her arms dropped to her sides in defeat, her face going pale. She had failed in her mission, a mission to bend the leader of her enemy to her will. She had beguiled the wrong man. "What does this clan chief want? What could we possibly have that he needs?"

Khalvir shook his head. "Have you not figured it out?" he spat. "Do you still cling to the notion that my People pursue you for no other reason than to gobble you up? Are you so blind?" He shoved his hand with the fingers she had healed into her dazed and confused face. "He covets your witch power! I did not believe its wonders to be real until I witnessed it for myself. Few of us believed our Chief's stories. Now I understand his need." He touched his recently healed leg. "It is your own power that has put you in danger. My clan Chief will never stop until he possesses your skills for himself."

"W-what?" Now she looked faintly green. Khalvir stood and let the implications of his words sink in. She reached out to support herself against a rock wall. "I-I never thought, we j-just thought-." Her voice faded as she frowned. "B-but... if you didn't believe in our powers before... how did anyone else... why?"

Khalvir laughed bitterly. "It seems I was not the first to be healed by one of your kind, elf," he said. "My Chief has always told of how an elf witch brought him back from the brink of death. Spooked in the heat of the moment, he tried to cut the healer's throat, but the witch was too quick. My Chief only wounded his face. The Chief escaped and returned to his clan.

"But as the shock wore off, the memory of that elf festered. My Chief grew hungry to possess this power for his own People and started hunting your People in an effort to capture a live elf. He sought to capture women to breed with, in the hope they would pass on the gift to their offspring. We have taken many, but none of them ever survived away from their forests. They grew sick and failed."

Nyriaana's hands came up to cover her face, as if trying to block out the terrible truth he had just revealed to her. "I can't believe it," she whispered. "I can't..."

Khalvir wished he could take it back and ease her pain. His heart yearned for him to go to her. But he could not give in. Better this than the alternative. This truth would not shatter her. She would heal. But if his men captured her here with him, it would not be so.

And she did not truly care for him. The sting of betrayal tore through Khalvir again, and his voice was icy as he spoke. "Believe it. It is the truth. I am your mortal enemy and I will only bring you death. I am sworn to obey my Chief. I never was your Juaan. I am Khalvir. Now leave before—"

Khalvir did not get to speak further. One moment she was standing and the next her knees were buckling from under her. Agony ripped across her face. He was at her side in an instant, his tenuous control shattering as she toppled forwards, clutching at her chest. Horrified, he caught her before she hit the ground. "What is it? What's wrong?"

"I have to go," she rasped. "I have to go." She pushed away as she shot to her feet and ran from him. Without a backward glance, she scrambled up the rope and was gone.

He had done it. He had driven her away. Khalvir knew instinctively that the witch would never return. "I'm sorry," he called softly, knowing she would not hear, then sank to his knees and let the grief have him.

***

CHAPTER 19

RETURN

A whistle split the air across the plains. Galahir leaped to his feet, dimly aware that the men around the campfire had done the same. All except Banahir, who remained seated.

"Lorhir!" Ranab exclaimed. "Lorhir is returning."

Relief uncoiled the knot in Galahir's gut. One way or the other, the wretched wait was over. Galahir did not think he could have borne the tension for even one more day. He tightened his grip around his *arshu*, wondering if the Chief had sent Lorhir back with reinforcements.

Utu was almost at her zenith when the sharp-eyed Banahir sounded the alert. "There!"

Galahir strained his eyes into the distance. It took him a moment before he picked out the single figure wavering on the line between earth and sky. Lorhir. The tall, whip-like form was unmistakable. For a handful of heartbeats, Galahir feared that the other warrior was alone, and they were to be ordered back to the clan, but then a second figure appeared, then another and another, until five more men lined the horizon at Lorhir's back. Two were carrying something large between them.

Whoops and welcoming whistles went up from the group around the campfire. Galahir kept his eyes away from them. Never had he witnessed such a greeting for the usually despised Lorhir. He, Galahir, had done that, so poor had he proven in leadership. His cheeks flamed afresh.

Lorhir's face glowed as he absorbed the attention upon entering camp. The large object two of the other men had been carrying was the carcass of a half grown ox calf, which they slammed down next to the fire in triumph.

Sick to the stomach, Galahir could barely bring himself to look at the thin man. Lorhir had no such compunctions. He smirked in Galahir's direction, making a pointed sweep of the camp with his eyes, emphasising the fact that Khalvir was still absent from their number.

"Still no sign of the other half-breed, then?" he taunted.

Galahir ignored him. "What orders do you bring?" he asked dully.

Lorhir grinned. "The Chief has placed *me* in charge of this raiding party. We are to attack the elven settlement and take as many prisoners as we can, as Khalvir failed to do. I hope you haven't been idle, Galahir."

Galahir studied the reinforcements accompanying Lorhir. All carried twice the amount of weaponry than those the Chief had sent Khalvir with. A fact Lorhir appeared to be overlooking.

It would do no good to point this out, however. Instead, Galahir let the elation of knowing that they would enter the forest again temper the sting of Lorhir's insults. This was exactly the outcome he had been hoping for. He lifted his chin. "I know where to find the settlement. I can lead you there."

"Good." Lorhir's face twisted into a smile before snapping his fingers in Galahir's face. "Now, make yourself useful and clean that carcass for me. Once we have feasted and recovered from our journey, we will enter the forest at nightfall."

Galahir lowered his head in acknowledgement, ignoring the sniggers that had erupted around the campfire as he drew his hunting knife and crouched obediently beside the dead beast.

Tonight. One last chance. As he had sat brooding upon the outskirts of the camp for the past days, his mind had not been idle. He had been re-running all that he had learned about the forest in his head.

He would lead Lorhir to the elven settlement, but he would not take the most direct route. There was one remaining area he had not yet covered in his searches. One more area, one more hope.

He prayed to all the gods that this time Khalvir would answer.

***

Chapter 20

BETRAYAL

Utu rose and set and Khalvir remained alone. He considered letting himself die in this place. Her absence was a wound in his heart that would not heal; the thought that he would not see her again an agony that he could not contain. He lay unfeeling upon the cold, hard ground, unable to bring himself to look at the shelter they had made, much less enter it. He had known true love for the first time and had the illusion of that love being returned. Now Khalvir did not know how he would live without it. He slept fitfully.

When the first whistle sounded, he ignored it. He did not care. If they did not find him, maybe they would leave.

Stop, a voice in his head told him, *you are* raknari, *your People still need you. Survival is everything.*

Survival was everything. The ebbing flame of Khalvir's heart flickered, rousing him. His own feelings did not matter. He had a duty to his People. His life might have lost all meaning, but he was still alive and his life could save theirs one day. That was his purpose. A sad sigh found its way past his lips. It was time to abandon the magic. It was time to go home.

When the next whistle sounded, Khalvir answered mournfully. The thrilling reply came from the distance, acknowledging him, and Khalvir fancied he detected a note of relief in the answer.

The sudden rustling of leaves and branches jolted Khalvir from his concentration. *No!* His heart leapt as dread filled him. She had come *back*.

But it was not Nyriaana's face that greeted him as the coverings of his prison were pulled asunder. Khalvir stepped back as a man peered down at him with a weary expression. His red-gold skin was lined beneath his silvery white hair. Khalvir experienced the oddest thrill of familiarity. He knew at the centre of his being that he should know this man, though he could not understand why.

"So it is true," the stranger whispered.

Khalvir eyed the intruder.

"I had my suspicions," the older man continued to murmur. It was clear he was talking to himself and was not addressing Khalvir.

"Who are you?" Khalvir demanded.

"That does not matter," the stranger replied

"Then what do you want?" Khalvir growled. He was tired and in no mood for any more games. He just wanted to be left alone.

"To look on you with my own eyes and see for myself what you have become."

Khalvir barked a laugh. "And what do you see, may I ask?"

"Everything that I ever feared."

Khalvir tightened his fists. "Just leave me in peace," he ground out through his teeth.

"Nyriaana has been coming here, hasn't she?"

The sound of her name sent another unpleasant thrill through him. Khalvir pressed his lips together, though he wasn't sure why he should protect her secret.

But the stranger lifted his chin, Khalvir's silence was apparently all the confirmation he needed. "You always were her greatest weakness, same as her mother, same as... your mother. Nyriaana is the only one to have survived you, now you have returned to threaten her life, yet again."

Agony ripped from somewhere deep inside Khalvir's chest at the witch's words. The pain of it was astonishing. "*Leave!*" He stooped to pick up a rock, unable to bear another word.

"You are going to betray her. That was you calling, wasn't it, you are bringing your men."

"Yes." Khalvir saw no point in denying it.

"I thought as much. Just know that it is my duty to protect her."

Sudden recognition hit as Khalvir's eyes lighted on the long scar marring the elf's jawbone. *Baarias.* Now he knew why the name was so familiar to him in more ways than one. He had heard it uttered from his own Chief's mouth. This was the very healer who was responsible for it all. Nyriaana's own teacher. Now he had the advantage. He would wipe the superior look off this man's face.

"Are you going to tell her?" he asked coolly.

"Tell her what?"

"Tell her you betrayed her far worse than I ever could. Are you going to admit how you were the one who healed my Chief and in doing so brought about the destruction of everything she holds dear."

Khalvir's words struck their target, his deductions proving correct. This was the one. Fury and pain twisted the lined face. The healer composed himself with an effort. "It matters not," he said. "Just know that I will do what I must. Her life means more to me than anything else, more than my own."

Khalvir nodded, accepting the threat. He didn't need to say more. This man knew what he had done. He wondered if Nyriaana would turn from him when she learned the truth. He hoped so. That would be his just punishment.

It appeared that Baarias had tired of his visit. He turned away. "Good-bye, sister-son," he murmured so softly that Khalvir could not be certain of the words. He replaced the leaves, leaving Khalvir once again in darkness.

Khalvir paced the small space, waiting impatiently for his fate to find him. He was under no illusions as to what the old man had meant by his words. He would kill Khalvir to protect Nyriaana if he had to. Meanwhile, the whistles of his men were getting nearer. It would not be long now. Either Baarias would send the elven tribe to finish him or his own men would come. One way or another, he would be out of this pit by daybreak. It was just a matter of who would get to him first. He didn't really care which. He folded himself into a corner and waited.

At last they came.

"Khalvir! Where are you?" He could hear footsteps above.

"Galahir!" he called back. "Down here."

He heard a faint cry of surprise.

"Watch your step," Khalvir cautioned. "The ground is treacherous."

His imprisonment was over. He would go back to his life, free of these walls. Or at least his body would escape. His heart would remain here. He knew he would miss her for the rest of his days. He hoped she was safe now, wherever she was.

Galahir pulled the coverings back from the pit. "We've slipped by their sentries unseen, we've been testing them for days. It's almost impossible to evade them. We need to be quick before we are discovered."

Khalvir rose to his feet. Then he paused as something niggled against his senses. He concentrated harder, focusing as she had taught him. Someone was coming. His heart clenched in sudden fear.

"Get out of here!" he hissed up to Galahir. "Go! Do nothing until I call!"

Galahir's broad face showed alarm, but he knew to obey the tone in Khalvir's voice. His friend disappeared from view.

The presence was getting nearer, running through the undergrowth. Khalvir's heart pounded in his chest, heavy with dread. If she had come back, even after everything he had said, he didn't know how he would stop his men from taking her captive.

A face appeared in the opening Galahir had just made. But it was not her face. It was not even Baarias. This face was new. A young male face. Khalvir noted the angular, birdlike bone structure, the dark hair, the red-gold skin, so similar to Nyriaana's own. This man must be her close kin. But unlike her beloved face, this one was twisted into the expression that he had long ago come to associate with one of his kind.

Hatred.

Khalvir coiled his muscles, lips curling back off his teeth. Baarias had wasted no time.

"So, Juaan, we meet again," the latest stranger hissed. "I was told I would find you here. I hardly dared to believe my luck and yet here you are, offered up to me like a gift from Ninmah herself."

Again with the *Juaan*. Khalvir glared up at the stranger. "And who are you?"

A smile twisted over the cruel face, and Khalvir felt another shiver of distant recognition curl in his stomach. It was not a pleasant sensation.

"Surely you remember me? Daajir. The boy you so delighted in tormenting so long ago."

Daajir! Khalvir tensed at the mention of the hated name. Here was the one who had attacked Nyriaana.

And then, as if his very thoughts had summoned her, Khalvir heard her voice come screaming through the trees. "*Daajir!* No! Leave him alone!"

Khalvir closed his eyes in despair. All his efforts had been for nothing. There was no way to prevent what was going to happen now, and he did not see how he was going to live through it. He should never have called his men. He should have curled up and died here. He just hoped he would have the chance to see the hated figure gloating above him lying dead at his feet.

Khalvir gathered his energy. Driven by rage, it leaped eagerly to his grasp. He prepared to unleash it, to let it do what it would to the elf witch above.

"I promised I would see you dead one day, Forbidden," Daajir said, drawing Khalvir's own knife into view. A dark liquid stained the dripping tip. "Now I finally get the opportunity I thought robbed from me all those Furies ago." The witch drew back his arm, preparing to throw. Khalvir bared his teeth and readied himself to release the energy inside him.

"Nyri! Stop!"

And suddenly she was there. Khalvir watched, frozen in shock, as she smashed Daajir around the back of the head with a rock. Once, twice. The knife dropped from the now limp fingers as Daajir crumpled to the ground.

Nyriaana stood over her fallen kin, trembling from head to foot as blood dripped from the rock in her hand, but her eyes were resolute. "I'm sorry," she whispered to him. "I am so sorry."

Khalvir could not respond. He locked away his heart to protect himself from what was to come.

"Nyri." Baarias appeared, his voice full of consternation as he dropped to his knees beside the heap that was Daajir. "What have you *done*?"

Nyri did not even look at her teacher as she threw the now well used root over the edge. "Come on," she rasped.

Khalvir unlocked his muscles and grabbed hold of the root, controlling his breathing as he pulled himself up, searching for the strength he needed. He was a *raknari* of his clan, bound to obey and serve his Chief. If he showed the slightest weakness, his men would turn on him. He climbed out of the hated pit and stood before her, free at last.

Khalvir's resolve was tested as she threw her arms around him and held him tight. Numb inside, he tried to commit the feel of her body against his to memory, her warmth, her scent. For this was the last time she would hold him so.

All too soon she pulled away, her expression telling him how much effort it took to let him go. "Go!" she sobbed. "Go, get away from here! Leave!"

Khalvir did not move. He stood still as a stone before her. She did not understand yet, the horror that awaited.

"What are you waiting for?" She pushed him. "*Go!*"

There was just time for one last touch. Khalvir reached out his fingers to stroke her cheek. Nyriaana closed her eyes and leaned into his hand.

"I can't," he whispered. The moment of shattering had come. He had done all he could, but he could protect her no longer. She belonged to his Chief now. Khalvir withdrew his hand.

"Why not?" she demanded. "Leave me! They'll kill you! You need to go. I have given you your freedom!"

"You have." Khalvir stared down into the eyes that he loved. His voice was dead. "But I said nothing about being able to give you yours. I told you you should have left me to die. It would have been better for the both of us."

"W-what?" she choked, still oblivious, still trusting. "What do you mean? L-leave now, while you still can. I can't see you hurt."

"Nyri! Get away from him!" Baarias cried, understanding what she did not.

"I am so very sorry," Khalvir said and whistled out to the waiting Galahir.

Nyriaana did not take her gaze from his as Galahir and the rest re-materialised out of the darkness, forcing Khalvir to witness the very moment the light went out of her eyes.

Ranab came forward to seize her arm, and she did not resist as she continued to stare into Khalvir's face.

"You!" Baarias was suddenly on his feet, rushing for him. "You will not take her!"

Lorhir reacted immediately. Before Khalvir could stop him, he had thrown his spear. The weapon caught the older elf high in the chest, throwing him to the ground with a soft gasp as the breath left his body.

"Lorhir, stop!" Khalvir snarled as a very familiar silver-haired she-elf burst from concealment. She threw herself to the fallen man's side, hands growing bloody as she wrapped them around the spear.

From the corner of his eye, Khalvir watched Nyri's knees buckle at the sight of her fallen teacher. Only Ranab's grip on her arm kept her upright.

I'm so sorry.

"Are there more of them close by?" Galahir whispered to Khalvir.

"Yes," Khalvir answered, not even realising he was still using the elven tongue in his numb state. "Yes, they are all in the settlement.

Nanna is fully awake. They will not venture far." He made a hand gesture, directing them into the trees.

Ranab dropped Nyri's arm in his eagerness to obey. She did not have the strength to hold herself up, and she collapsed to the ground. Khalvir's throat tightened at the sight of it.

"No." She crawled on her hands and knees to kneel at his feet. His own knees trembled, and he locked them in place. "No please," she beseeched. "No please. Take me. Just me. Leave my People. I'm a healer. I am everything your People want. Please. Grant me this one thing. Leave my family be. I-I'll do whatever you a-ask." She clutched at his furs in anguish.

"You will die out there." Khalvir heard rather than felt the words fall from his lips.

"Please. Please."

And he could not do it. Even for his own life. Her hold on him was too strong. He was ruined. "What *is* it about you?" he murmured to her, then raised his head and damned himself to his fate. "Leave her People."

His men turned to him, startled. Lorhir pulled the concealing skull from his face, revealing features twisted with rage. "You would disobey the orders of your own Chief! You-"

Fury surged through Khalvir's limbs as he unleashed his pain and anger upon Lorhir. He struck out with his fist, catching the hated man across the nose before he could even blink. The bone crunched satisfyingly on impact.

"I said, *leave* her People." But Khalvir knew that was all that was in his power. She had admitted her skill to his men. Lorhir understood the elf tongue almost as well as he did. If Khalvir did not take her now, they would turn on him. "This one is valuable enough. Take her and the other girl. Leave the old man. He won't make it."

Galahir moved to pull the silver-haired girl away from her fallen kinsman.

"No!" Nyri rasped. "Please. Just me."

Be still, you fool. You have already sealed both our dooms. He glared at her. "I have done all I can for you. Be silent and ask no more. Accept if you are to live."

Her fate was now in his Chief's hands.

Khalvir turned his back on her and walked away without another glance. He was free. But he knew his freedom was a lie. He was still captive. There had been a time when he had believed the pit would become his tomb. Khalvir could not have guessed then that it would become the tomb for his own heart. A heart he was leaving further behind with every step he took.

The night closed around Khalvir's soul and did not let go.

***

THE END

Continue your journey through time with *Enemy Tribe, Book 3 of THE ANCESTORS SAGA*

Also by Lori Holmes

Printed in Great Britain
by Amazon